LETHAL CARGO

LETHAL CARGO

Mike Lowe

FEEDAREAD

www.feedaread.com

Published in 2022 by FeedARead Publishing

A CIP catalogue record for this title is available from the British Library.

Set in 11-point Palatino Linotype

For my very good friend, Clive, for agreeing to be a character in the story

Also by Mike Lowe

Milvar's Path
Going Dutch
Hermit
Banger
LoGO
All at Sea
All Risks
The Curator
Treasures - (including Monk's Gold)
So Many Paths (autobiography)

1

Paul Thomas, recently retired journalist, lived at number one Fishers' Lane, in the little fishing village of Hildisham, North Norfolk. His tiny red brick and flint cottage was one of a row built in the eighteenth century to house the crews of the fishing fleet.

Paul bought the house when he married Laura Singleton, a graphic designer. Laura had decorated the little dwelling and furnished it, adding paintings and ornaments to make it a cosy and stylish home.

While on what was supposed to be the holiday of a lifetime in Turkey, visiting all the historic sites such as Ephesus and Hattusa - the great city of the Hittites, and the Colossus of Memnon, as well as enjoying the sunshine, Laura had contracted a viral infection.

Despite being flown home promptly, and given the best medical care, she had not been able to fight the toxins. She died, leaving Paul devastated. He was still not able to come to terms with his loss.

Soon after Laura's death, a devastating fire had destroyed all but the two end cottages in the lane. The space in between the houses, that now looked like bookends, had been made into allotments after a proposed development had been turned down by an unusually sensible town council.

Paul had contemplated moving if the building had gone ahead. But deep down he knew he could never leave. He loved the little cottage and its memories. Everything about the house reminded him of his wife.

Paul's nearest neighbours, the Stevensons, lived a hundred yards away, at the other end of the lane. Still near enough to help when the need arose, such as looking after Mr Brown, his old tabby cat, when he was away on assignments. But sadly, the old cat had died. The animal had been the last link to Laura, leaving him with nobody to talk to but himself. He no longer had occasion to talk to the kindly couple at the end of the lane, although if he had admitted it, he did need to talk to them.

He had almost become a recluse. He sought solace in drink, often consuming a whole bottle of whiskey a day.

After almost a year, in which his only comfort was alcohol, Paul had returned to his work, writing for whichever magazine or newspaper that would give him an assignment, and often finding stories himself and selling them to the highest bidder.

He had been successful, and made a good living despite the dangers the job very often put him in. With nobody but himself to worry about he had often gone headlong into dangerous situations.

Several times he had involved friends in his work, notably, Richard Allen who in their last adventure together had lost his beloved motor-torpedo-boat and still blamed Paul for it.

Finding it increasingly difficult to find suitable stories, Paul had decided to call it a day and settle down, using his experiences to write novels.

After years of chasing after stories for the magazine and getting involved in all manner of dangerous situations, with and without his friend Richard, Paul was looking forward to a quiet life. He had often toyed with the idea of writing; he certainly had enough experiences to call upon. Yet when he sat at his desk, poised to begin writing, nothing had come, he couldn't even think how to start.

He could write a formal report or a factual account, he could dress up an account to make it readable and acceptable to the editor of a magazine – he'd been doing that for years, he was after all a journalist, but somehow, he was unable to write fiction.

He was finding it difficult to cope with so much leisure time. He was on his own again after the latest of his young lady-friends had found him too difficult to live with.

He was finding himself difficult to live with, and once more a dark depression had descended on him and he had taken to drink again. It had been two or three weeks so far this time and the longer it went on the harder it would be to stop.

He knew very well the consequences of drinking a bottle of whiskey a day, but he couldn't stop himself. A bottle of Jamieson's, the last of a case brought over from Ireland, stood on the kitchen table, temptingly. Something moved him to try to resist. He put the bottle in a cupboard, right at the back, so he couldn't see it when he opened the door.

'I'm not going to have a drink today,' he promised himself, making a pot of tea instead.

'And I won't have one tomorrow, see how it goes.'

He went to the frig and remembered he didn't have any milk.

He took his cup of black tea into the living room and sat sipping it as he sifted through the day's post. His hands shook as he tore open the envelopes, discarding them and adding the contents to an untidy pile.

When all the envelopes had been opened, he began to look at the contents. Most were advertising some quack medical product or other and were quickly discarded. Ever since he had bought an arthritis remedy from one of these quasi-medical companies, he had been bombarded with adverts for cures for every condition imaginable. The arthritis remedy had been very expensive and had not helped at all.

'Bloody quacks!' he grumbled.

Two more were bills, which he also dismissed. One was a statement of his pension; it didn't amount to much, but it helped. He was still not old enough to receive the state pension. He would have to live off his meagre savings until he could think of a way of generating income.

The next letter was from Lucy Templeton, one of Laura's old friends, kindly asking how he was.

'I'm bloody miserable, if you must know! Why can't people just leave me alone?' he blurted out.

The truth was that he was desperately lonely and needed people, but he could not see it.

Leaving the remainder of his post, he wandered aimlessly into his tiny kitchen.

'What did I come in here for?' he muttered. 'Oh! I know, a drink, where did I put that bottle?'

He opened the cupboard door and reached in, but something stopped him.

'No, not today. I'm sober today,' he said out loud, then humming tunelessly he returned to the living room and the pile of post.

'Get a grip, man. For God's sake. You'll go crazy if you're not careful.' He was talking to himself a lot lately, and not always in English.

There was still a lucid mind trying to break through and he began to take stock of his situation.

Promising not to drink and being able to resist the temptation was the first step.

He looked at the rest of the post.

A brochure from a publisher, a reminder from the dentist to make an appointment, a free ticket to a new gym, a magazine about beer, which in a rash moment he had asked for in an online advertisement.

He pushed the pile to one side and finished his tea, which had gone cold.

The letter from Laura's friend had started him thinking of his wife again. His beautiful wife, cut off cruelly in her prime. They had been blissfully happy and all Paul's problems related to her death. He knew he could never get over her loss; he had tried, and had some pleasant liaisons with young women that had taken his mind off his grief for a while, but the memories of his wife always came flooding back at the slightest provocation.

He smiled at the memory of the day Laura brought home her TR7.

'Hello, Darling, look what I've got! Come and see!' She had come in with all the enthusiasm of a child on Christmas morning. She had pulled Paul outside where a very sad looking pale blue sports car was parked on the patch of gravel in front of the garage that Laura liked to call the drive.

'It'll be fine, don't worry,' said Laura, quickly, seeing Paul's expression. 'I've found a firm near Royston, in Hertfordshire and they are going to do it up for me. It'll be lovely, you'll see!' She was breathless in her haste to explain before Paul had a chance to say anything.

'Well, I suppose if you like it . . . '

'I do, it's a Triumph TR7 and it will be beautiful when it's had the treatment.'

In due course and at considerable expense, the car had been fully restored and had extras fitted to bring it up to modern standards. Paul thought it was ugly, and it wasn't a proper TR, but he had to be pleased with his wife's enthusiasm for it.

When Laura died, Paul had not been able to part with the car, he kept it well maintained and enjoyed driving it. He had even begun to like its unusual looks.

Paul's tears were running down his face unhindered as he remembered his wife's happy and childlike enthusiasm. The memory was good, but it hurt. But somehow the hurt was good, too.

Hauling himself painfully from his chair and scattering the pile of post in the process, Paul made his way to the garage where the TR7 was parked alongside his motorbike, a gleaming black, Triumph Speed Triple 1050R. Paul loved the machine and would never consider parting with it, although these days he rarely rode it.

But it was Laura's car that he had come to see. He opened the driver's door and slid into the sumptuous leather seat, holding the leather covered rim of the steering wheel taken from a TR8. Sitting in the car he felt close to Laura. He smiled at the memory.

The leather seats were not original, nor was the electronic ignition or the fuel injection or the specially tuned stainless steel exhaust system, or its gleaming Connaught Green paintwork.

The purists at the club had criticized the improvements Laura had made to the car, saying the car was no longer original and therefore not eligible to be entered in concours events. But Paul didn't mind that. The alterations were Laura's and that made it special.

As he sat in the dark snug cockpit of the car that had been so precious to his wife, he was able to separate himself from his feelings of hopelessness for a moment or two. Memories took him away and into a happier time. After a while he slept and began to dream . . .

2

The Dream

Not sure what he was looking for, Paul parked the little Peugeot 208 hire car and locked it.

The houses in the lane looked downtrodden and in need of repair. Some roofs were made of corrugated iron sheets, roughly placed so that the edges overhung the walkway precariously. There was debris of all sorts on the ground. There was not a soul about and it was very quiet.

Paul walked slowly and carefully, avoiding the most unpleasant looking rubbish.

A shop, with its produce spilling out onto the walkway was selling meat and vegetables, swarms of flies were buzzing round the display; the smell was nauseating. Paul hurried past.

Narrow alleyways either side of the main walkway looked dark and dangerous to Paul, though he couldn't have said why he felt that way.

He looked again at the scrap of paper on which was written a name and address. Surely this can't be right, he thought. 'Conrad Espanieri, 17, Avenue des Artistes.' If only there was someone he could ask.

He kept walking until he came to a stretch of muddy water in which a group of young women were washing clothes. *Where on earth am I?* thought Paul, not for the first time.

Cautiously approaching the women, he asked, 'Do you know this address?' and showed the piece of paper.

The women cowed away from him and hid their faces.

'I mean you no harm,' Paul persisted as one of the women got up and ran down a side alley.

'I don't like this at all', thought Paul. But he continued along the walkway, hoping to find someone who could help him.

The walkway opened up into a small square with what looked like shops on three sides. The fourth side was taken up by an open-fronted building in which he could see men apparently sorting through piles of clothes. A first floor was also visible and there were men piling mattresses onto a flatbed truck. 'How did the truck get up there?' he wondered.

He called out, 'Hello! Can anyone help me?'
The men showed no sign of having heard him, so he called again. 'I'm looking for Conrad Espanieri!'

One of the men sorting clothes came out and faced Paul. 'Conrad Espanieri?'

'That's right. Do you know where I can find him?'

The man looked Paul in the eye and came very close. Paul backed off.

'Conrad Espanieri,' the man said again.

'Yes, do you know where he lives?'

'No estoy de acuerto, Señor. Espanieri est muerde.'

Paul had learned Spanish years ago when he had been a regular visitor to Spain and although it had been a long time since he had spoken it, he understood what the man was saying. Espanieri was death! What had he got himself into this time?

'Gracias, Señor,' said Paul, backing away from the man, who turned and returned to his work.

'I can't give in now,' he thought. 'I must find this guy, otherwise I'll be in trouble.'

He continued in the direction he had been walking, at least he thought it was the same direction. The buildings here were bigger and even more dilapidated. They looked like factories, but there was no indication what they might produce. There was no sound of machinery and no smoking chimneys.

The alley came to a dead end. The door to a dwelling was open but there seemed to be nobody about. He could see through the house and it looked as if the path continued the other side. He went in. There was no one in sight, but there was a smell of cooking, someone was not far away. He hurried on, not wanting to confront anyone.

The path was no better the other side, and there were still no people about.

By now, Paul was feeling very uneasy. He had no idea where he was or indeed where he was going. He had to try *to find this man even if he was death. If he didn't pick up the package, he was afraid of what might happen.*

Suddenly, two men – large, intimidating men - appeared in front of Paul. He stopped and smiled.

There was no returned smile.

'Er, do you know where I can find Conrad Espanieri?' he asked quietly.

'Espanieri! What you want with him?' the biggest man asked, in thickly accented English.

'I have to pick up a package from him,' said Paul, hoping he had not said too much.

'A package, eh?' the man looked at his companion, who smiled evilly.

'Yes, do you know where I can find him?'

'You must be very careful, Señor, he is dangerous man,' the first man spoke in a more friendly tone now, and even managed a smile, showing irregular and discoloured teeth.

'Yes, thank you, but do you know where I can find him?'

'He lives in the big house at the end of the road, Camino de los Artistas. Número diecisiete.'

'Thank you very much. And where is that exactly?'

The other man was gesturing to his friend to come away.

'Keep going, Señor, you will find it,' said the man, and he turned and walked away.

Paul was getting more and more uneasy as he continued into the depths of the town where the buildings were so poor, they looked uninhabitable, and yet there were people in them. More smells of cooking filled the air and it was getting warmer.

A larger building came into view. 'The man said look for a large building; is this it?' Paul wondered.

The sign on the corner of the building read, 'Camino de los Artistas.'

'This looks like it,' he muttered, wondering why the address had been given to him in French. Looking at the door of the largest building – they said the big house.

Beautiful calligraphy in white paint read, Número diecisiete. Why don't they use numerals? What's that? Is that seventeen?' He had never been sure about Spanish numbers but guessed it must be seventeen. He raised the ornate knocker, and let it fall. 'This feels all wrong,' he thought.

A few minutes passed and Paul considered knocking again, but then suddenly the door opened and an attractive young woman was standing there, smiling.

'Señor?'

'Oh, Permítanme hablar con, 'Señor Espanieri.'

I can still remember some Spanish,' he thought.

'Si, Señor, Por supuesto por favor, espere aquí un momento.'

'Gracias,' said Paul, guessing she had said to wait.

A few more minutes later an elderly man, dressed in a dark suit that might have been fashionable a hundred years ago, came to the door. He smiled, and gestured for Paul to enter.

'I imagine you would prefer to speak English, Señor. You have come to pick up a small package that I would like you to deliver to an address in England. I understand you have agreed to this, yes?'

'Yes, that's right. May I ask what is in the package?'

'You may ask, of course, but I cannot tell you. For one reason, you would not understand, and also it is better you do not know. What I can tell you is that the package does not contain anything dangerous. It will not however be permitted to pass through customs, so you must take precautions. Do you understand?'

'Yes,' said Paul.

'Very well, then here it is.' The man produced a small rectangular box from his pocket. 'Be careful, it is very heavy.' He handed the box to Paul.

Paul was surprised how heavy the box was. He guessed that perhaps it contained gold. That would probably weigh this much.

'Now, perhaps you would like some refreshment before you go?'

'Thank you, I would, it took me a long time to find you.' This man they call death seems very civilised and pleasant, he thought.

When he had finished a plate of tiny sandwiches and a glass of wine, served by the young woman, he left. Espanieri called, 'Via con Dios,' as he stepped out into the sunshine.

Nothing seemed real. It was disturbing.   Hoping he was retracing his steps; he began to walk away.

He examined the box carefully. There appeared to be no lid and no hinges, nor was there a lock. It was made of a close-grained wood, probably mahogany he thought. It had been nicely finished and was pleasant to touch. He stroked the surface wondering what could be inside. He shook it gently. Whatever was inside fitted well, there was no movement.

He had not been looking where he was going. He realised with horror that he didn't recognise any of the buildings.

'I need to find someone to ask the way', he thought, but then, 'the way to what?' He had no idea where he wanted to go. Back to the hotel, but where was that. He couldn't remember its name or even the name of the little town.

It was getting dark and the buildings began to show lights. Cooking smells still filled the air. Sounds of talking from the buildings but no sign of people.

He pressed on, desperately hoping to see something he recognised. It all looked different. He began to think he was going mad. His heart was beating unnaturally fast and he was breathing in short gasps. His feet were unsteady.

A young woman came out of one of the houses and seeing Paul, exclaimed, 'Señor, está bien? Necesitas ayuda?'

'She was asking if he needed help, Paul asked if she knew the way out of the town. He spoke in English but the woman understood. She took his arm and gently turned him towards an opening he hadn't seen. She pointed and said, 'Vaya por este camino, Señor, no está lejos.'

'Gracias, Señorita, molto gracias.'

The woman smiled and waved as Paul set off in the direction she had indicated.

Very soon the buildings thinned out and he could see cars. Was it the car park? That would be too much to hope for. He hurried on and he could see that it was indeed a car park. But was it the one where he had left the little Peugeot? He wished he had been driving something more easily recognisable. All the cars looked similar. He couldn't remember the registration of the hire car. He looked through the windows of several small Peugeots and then, Heaven be praised, he saw his jacket on the seat of one of them. He pressed the key fob and the car clicked and the lights flashed.

His cry of thanks to God was genuine.

When Paul woke, he was breathing hard and he was sweating. He continued to sit in the car for a few minutes to get his breath back. The dream had been disturbing. He'd never had a dream like it before. He could not explain it – he couldn't describe it. It was so bizarre and surreal. He had total recall; its horror was still with him. But it was over. At least he hoped it was. He almost expected to see the box still in his hands.

Vowing once more to stop drinking, he shook his head, trying to erase the memory.

He climbed unsteadily from the car and returned to the house. He made himself a cup of coffee, strong and black, but did not add the usual slug of whiskey, even though there was an unopened bottle of Jamieson's in the cupboard.

3

The dream had been so worrying he could not get it out of his mind. But strangely, he felt better. He saw the dream as an allegory. He was lost, but the dream suggested to him that although Laura was no longer with him, he did still have people to whom he could turn for help, or perhaps even comfort.

He suddenly realised he was hungry. He hadn't eaten properly for some time; he couldn't remember the last proper meal he'd had.

There was no food in the house so he thought about ordering a takeaway, but then decided to go into the village; fish and chips perhaps, in one of the restaurants on the quayside.

He had not ventured out of the house for weeks and he hadn't washed or showered in all that time. His beard, a straggly looking thing, would take a few more weeks before becoming acceptable, but no matter, he was going to get himself out of his slough of despond. He actually felt good.

He had given up wearing his watch so had no idea of the time. He had spotted the watch, a Rolex Oyster, in a local auction a year or so ago, and perhaps because nobody appreciated its value it had been knocked for a silly price. He had been thrilled with his purchase, but lately there was no need to know what the time was. It was pitch dark outside, there were no lights showing in his neighbours' house at the end of the lane, so it must be late. He switched on the television and caught the end of the ten o'clock news. Not too late to eat.

It's only a short walk from Paul's house to Hildisham quay; it was a fine evening, perfect.

Several people looked disapprovingly at Paul when he entered the 'Good Plaice' fish restaurant, but the waiter didn't turn a hair, he did however show him to a table near the back.

Fish and chips in a restaurant less than twenty yards from the quay where the fish had been landed earlier in the day from the prime fishing grounds of the North Sea; what could be better?

His mood was getting better by the minute as his meal arrived – a piece of battered fish so big it overhung the sides of the plate, and the chips, freshly fried, crisp and golden, made his mouth water. He enjoyed the food immensely.

Feeling full, he refused a sweet and coffee; he left the restaurant and walked along the quay, admiring the fishing boats and pleasure craft moored there. The tide was in so the decks of the boats were almost level with the quay. There were still a few people enjoying the mild evening air and the atmosphere of this historic little quayside. Paul nodded to several crew members of the two remaining fishing boats who were enjoying a break from their hard and dangerous work, and he smiled at a young woman who was sitting on the aft deck of a sea-going cruiser, drinking something warming no doubt,

Just as he was about to call it a night and head for home, a car drove into the car park. Paul stopped to look at it. It was a Jaguar XK150, painted in British Racing Green. A real beauty.

'Don't see many of those,' quipped Paul to the driver as he climbed out of the car.

'No, you don't, just keep off, OK,' said the young man, gruffly.

Paul raised his hands in a gesture meaning that he would not dream of touching the car, but the young man did not respond, continuing towards the restaurant that Paul had just left.

It amused him to think that as he had been the last customer to be served before the restaurant's chef had gone home, this unpleasant man would be disappointed.

The old Jaguar got Paul thinking about classic cars again, and he wondered if something was telling him to get in touch with the guys at the car club. He had been made very welcome last time he'd been to a meeting, and it would be good to give the TR an outing.

As he made his way home, he wished he had thought to bring a torch. He almost missed his turning it was so dark. There was no moon and Norfolk County Council had not provided street lights in this end of the village. Another reference to being lost in his dream.

He was too tired when he got home to find out about the car club meeting so went straight to bed.

He slept well and when he woke the first thing that came into his head was to look up when and where the next meeting of the Triumph owners club would be held.

Even before getting dressed, he was rummaging through piles of paper, unanswered letters and unpaid bills on his desk in the tiny room he called his study. He knew there had been a newsletter from the club and it had to be there.

'Ahah!' he exclaimed, 'Here it is, what a filing system.' He smiled at his joke, and read the newsletter. The next meeting was going to be held in Sheringham, not too far away, on the first day of next month – May. 'Excellent – I'll go,' he said aloud.

4

The Links Country Park Hotel, near the sea-front in Sheringham, looked very grand. Its black and white exterior with red topped turrets was very distinctive.

Most of the spaces in the generous car park were filled with Triumph motor cars so Paul knew he had the right place. He slid the TR7 into a space between two TR3s. 'They won't like that,' he mused.

He made his way to the elegant conference room where the club was meeting. A sea of faces, and to begin with none that he recognised.

'Hello, Paul, old love, long time no see.' A portly middle-aged man with a large moustache, dressed in an old-fashioned velvet jacket and an embroidered yellow waistcoat was greeting Paul with a huge grin on his face. 'Are you OK? God, you look awful!'

'Oh, thanks,' muttered Paul, accepting the man's offered hand.

'Sorry, old man, bad form what? But it was a shock seeing you looking under par. Are you all right, really?'

Paul still could not place this escapee from a Bertie Wooster novel, but the man clearly knew him.

'I am OK, thanks, had a bit of a rough time, all good now though. How are you? I'm very sorry, I've forgotten your name.'

'All tickety-boo, old man, Henry Cartingdon-Bligh, once seen never forgotten surely, what?'

'Of course, I'm sorry, Henry,' Paul vaguely remembered the man although he had never had anything to do with him. 'What are you driving?'

'Got a Stag now, you'll remember me with a TR2, I expect. I found it too small, don't you know?' he said, gesturing to his ample stomach. 'And you, didn't you have a non-standard TR7?'

'I did indeed, and still have it. It belonged to my wife. Did you know Laura?'

'Of course, lovely gel, so sorry, old man.' He patted Paul's arm affectionately.

Paul warmed a little to the man, for all his theatrical manner he seemed genuinely sorry about Laura.

'Have you just arrived?' asked Henry, 'Have you seen any of the TR7 guys? They seem to keep themselves to themselves. They're over there, come on, let's go and see them.' Henry took Paul's elbow and led him towards a group of men, some of whom he recognised. Henry himself was absorbed into a crowd who appeared to be examining a piece of equipment.

'Hello, Paul!' exclaimed one of the men as Paul approached, 'haven't seen you for yonks, how's it going?'

Paul was pleased he remembered the man, 'Hello, Peter, it has been a long time, I'm sorry. I've had a bit of a rough time. I'm retired now, and things have been difficult. OK now though. How are you? You don't look any older!'

'Oh, you know, I'm OK, I've had few ups and downs, don't we all.' He laughed, but Paul sensed that some of the humour he remembered was lacking.

'Before we start the meeting, let me tell you, or I'll forget. Some of us are going on the *Rally de Carreras de Motor de Vall de Camprodon,*' he enunciated the foreign words carefully, – 'in Spain – do you know it? No, it's a kind of rally and we thought it would be fun. Do you want to come? It's next month. We're going *en-convoi*, stopping at as many drinking holes as possible on the way. It'll be a hoot. You with us?' He had spoken all in a breathless rush, slapping Paul's arm when he stopped.

The man's legendary enthusiasm had not left him, Paul was thinking.

'Well, it sounds intriguing, tell me more.'

Peter began to tell him more about the planned trip, but was interrupted by another club member, who dragged him away.

'I'll be back, Paul, think about it,' Peter called.

Just then, the club secretary stood up on a little dais and announced the programme for the evening and people began to move towards the seating area.

There was going to be a talk by an elderly man who had driven a TR3 all the way from Paris to Beijing – the classic veteran journey.

Paul took a seat alongside some of the TR7 guys and listened to the talk with interest.

In the interval, when most of the audience made for the bar, Paul left the TR7 guys; he didn't want to get involved in another drinking session.

Paul was finding socialising difficult, but having thought about it and argued with himself, he did decide to go to Spain. Peter Warburton had said they would be hosted by members of the *Club TR Register España* and there would only be the registration fees to pay. The understanding was that a reciprocal visit to England would be arranged later in the year. It sounded interesting and he thought it would do him good.

5

The group of about twenty club members, driving a variety of Triumph cars, met at the multi-story Port car park at Portsmouth, just a few yards from the Terminal building.

The mood was like that of a group of schoolchildren off on an adventure holiday. The original plan had been to take the shortest sea crossing and drive all the way through France to Spain, but in the end, they had opted to take the ferry to Santander and enjoy a longer sea voyage. The fact that drinks would be free on board was another incentive.

Once all the cars had been safely stowed on board, the club members began to congregate on deck.

'Hello, Paul, glad you could come,' said Peter, his customary grin lighting his face as he approached Paul. 'Looks as if we're in for a smooth crossing, I checked with the Met Office.'

'That's good, but I don't mind a rough sea myself,' said Paul. Although, if he was honest his memories of rough seas might have been enough to put him off seafaring for good. He was reminded of the time when his friend Richard's motor-torpedo-boat had been damaged in rough sea and then beached, never to sail again. Paul had promised to get him another boat, but never had. He still felt bad about it. Peter dragged him from his reverie.

'Oh, there's Henry; come on, let's join him and get some drinks in.'

Paul was not sure about Henry, but he had always got on well with Peter so he tagged along.

For a moment he thought, Henry - Harry, Spain, another link to his dream, but he quickly dismissed it from his mind.

Bob Lennox and Gus Stern joined them, and they found a table with a sea view, where another old friend, Trevor Truton was sitting.

'Can we get you a drink, Trev?' Peter asked as they sat down.

'What have they got?' asked Trevor.

'Mostly French lagers I expect, what do you fancy?' said Peter, 'I'll get 'em.'

'Don't mind, get a selection,' suggested Bob. 'All lagers taste the same tae me, anyway.'

'They laughed, but secretly the real ale drinkers agreed.

Peter came back from the bar with a tray laden with bottles. Paul chose Bière Spéciale, Bob grabbed a Brasserie and the others took the Heinekens.

Most of the group were regular attendees of club meetings, so knew each other very well; their conversation left Paul out.

Trevor seemed to be rather quiet. Paul, remembered that he had been in the Farina Club when they were investigating banger racing.

'I thought you were an Austin man, Trevor. Wasn't it a Westminster?'

'Yes, I still am! Well remembered. I still have the Westminster, but after meeting you Triumph types I bought myself a Roadster, I like a big car. I belong to both clubs now so I have a full calendar.'

'Did you get your car put right after that awful vandalism?'

'Oh, yes, of course. It cost me an arm and a leg to get it re-upholstered but it was worth it. She's a beauty. You've got a Seven, I believe.'

'Yes, that's right, it was my wife's car. She had it restored.'

'Didn't some of the guys complain that it wasn't standard?' asked Trevor, grinning.

Paul laughed, 'Yes, especially Peter, but I like the leather and the extras. It's not even a standard colour, Laura insisted on Connaught green.'

'Isn't that a BMC colour?'

'Yes, it is, she couldn't have annoyed the purists more if she had been trying!' he laughed.

'How funny, and leather you said? You can't beat leather can you? I love it.'

'You ready for another?' asked Gus, waving an empty bottle.

'Oh, lovely, thanks,' said Trevor. 'Do you want the same again, Paul?'

'Oh, might as well, it's OK,' he replied, smiling. 'Not like proper beer though, is it?' And not like drinking it out of a glass, either, he thought.

Paul bought the next round but drank slowly. He was reluctant to start drinking again.

Henry was talking very loudly and it was clear he'd had too much to drink already. Paul guessed he'd been adding spirits to his beer, or maybe drinking chasers.

Afraid he would be drawn into this drunken session, Paul excused himself and found a seat with a sea view, out of earshot of the club guys.

The motion of the boat was soporific and he soon slept, waking only when Peter prodded him and suggested getting something to eat.

'I had to get away, Peter, I'm sorry. I can't drink like you young chaps.'

'That's OK. I'm not so young now, I had to invent an excuse to leave myself. They make fools of themselves. They're like teenagers when they get together.'

'Where's the restaurant?'

'I've sussed it out, through there,' he pointed. 'The others are still drinking. They won't be fit to drive when we get to Santander. Idiots.'

When they were getting ready to disembark at Santander, it was clear that Henry was not fit to drive. Fortunately, Susan, the wife of one of the guys, kindly agreed to drive Henry's car to the hotel.

Members of the Spanish club were at the hotel to welcome them and the whole group dined together.

After a splendid meal and copious drinks, Henry was almost incapable of getting out of his seat. He was mumbling and spluttering in a most unpleasant manner. Several of the men decided to take him to his room to sober up. Paul helped.

They managed to get Henry partly undressed and into bed. One of the guys said he thought they should call an ambulance, as Harry seemed more than just drunk.

'Suppose he's had a stroke or something – he needs medical attention,' suggested a man Paul didn't know.

The others agreed and eventually an ambulance was called and Henry was taken to Hospital.

One of the guys phoned later to find out how Henry was. The doctor was conducting tests and would be able to tell them something later in the day.

It turned out that Henry had in fact had a stroke and was very poorly. Several of the chaps decided to visit him before the rally began.

Because Paul had been with the men who had taken care of Henry, he tagged along with them to the impressive-looking multi-storey hospital. The Marqués de Valdecilla-Santander University Hospital is in the centre of Santander and was easy to find.

Henry was sitting up in bed, but looking pale and wan.

There wasn't much any of them could say other than that they wished Henry well and looked forward to seeing him at the club.

Just as they were leaving, Henry called to Paul.

'Paul, come here old chap, there's a love.'

'Yes, what is it?' replied Paul cautiously, as he returned to Henry's bedside.

'I need you to do me a little favour, old dear,' he mumbled. 'I seem to have got myself in a bit of a mess. I'm likely to be here a while. I need you collect something for me. Just a little thing. Would you mind, only I'm not going to be able to make it.'

'What is it?' he asked, wondering why Henry had asked him.

'It's just a little gift for the lady wife. If you could pick it up for me, I would be very grateful. Look in the inside pocket of my jacket, bit of paper with the address. Good man, I knew I could rely on you.' And with that Henry closed his eyes and fell asleep, starting to snore almost immediately.

Not able to argue or refuse, Paul thought why not; he found Henry's clothes in a locker and rummaged in Henry's jacket for the piece of paper.

When he saw the name and address, a cold chill ran down his back and he had to sit down, staring in disbelief at the piece of paper.

Señor Estevan, Casa De La Musica, Avenida de la ópera, Torrelavega. Not so very different from the address in his dream. Or was he being melodramatic? It was nothing like the address in his dream, apart from the vaguely theatrical similarity. OK, so, better find out what Henry wants.

'What is it you want me to pick up, Henry?' he had to shake the man for a response.

'Wha? Oh, it's you, Paul, good man, good man. I would like to do me a little favour . . .'

'Yes, I know, what is it you want picking up?'

'Just a little parcel, dear boy. Take good care of it.' He closed his eyes again and it was clear he was not going to be able to tell Paul any more.

Paul left Henry and ran to catch up with the others who were headed back to their hotel.

He joined them in the bar where a group from the Spanish club were already well into another drinking session.

'Hola! Ven y únete a nosotros,' called one of the Spanish guys, 'Hablas español?'

Paul knew what he was saying come and join us, and did he speak Spanish, but although he did have a basic knowledge of the language, answered, 'No, sorry, not enough; do you speak English?'

It turned out that nearly all the Spanish guys could speak English very well. Paul, as usual felt ashamed of most of his countrymen's inability to learn languages.

'What's the plan?' Peter asked.

'The plan?' responded Manuel, who seemed to be the club's spokesman.

'The rally, tell us about it,' said Peter.

Oh si, of course,' Manuel went into a long, detailed explanation of the day's events and the rally that they had come for.

The first day would be for sightseeing, eating and drinking and the next day the cars would be examined and categorised. They would then be given details of the route. It all sounded very well organised.

Paul was wondering when he would find time to pick up Henry's parcel. He asked Manuel if Torrelavega was very far away.

'No, it is very close, just a few kilometres, why do you ask?'

'I have an errand to do for a friend.'

'An errand?'

'I have to pick something up for one of our party who is indisposed.'

'Indisposed?'

'Not very well.'

'Oh, I see, well, as I say, Torrelavega is not far away, maybe twenty kilometres, I will show you on the map.'

Having studied the map Paul could see that it would not take very long to get to Torrelavega. He reckoned he could be there and back before they had finished making the arrangements for the rally, and it was not due to start until the next day anyway.

6

Once Paul had left Santander, the countryside he drove through didn't look very different from that of England. The little villages had buildings that would look a little out of place in the UK, but somehow it didn't feel foreign.

It was good to have the car's top down and soak up the sunshine. He enjoyed the drive and had managed to push to the back of his mind thoughts about his disturbing dream.

Torrelavega is a pleasant town with well laid out streets and a variety of amenities. It looked to be a pleasant place to live. Paul had discovered that it had some very interesting history and its many old buildings and churches in particular bore this out. He was relieved to find no resemblance to his dream, that would have been too much to bear. He began to think how nice it would be to explore the place if he had time. But before he could think about anything else, he had to find **Señor Estevan**.

He parked the car in a small square and looked for someone to ask.

It was early afternoon and not many people were out and about. Like other Mediterranean countries, Spain is very quiet after lunch – Siesta time. He looked about and saw a building that could be an office of some kind. He went in. A reception desk with a young woman behind it looked promising. He tried his Spanish.

'Hola, disculpe, dónde está esta dirección?' he handed the scrap of paper with the address to the young woman. She looked at the paper, and at him. 'Are you English, Señor?'

'Yes, I'm sorry, did you not understand my Spanish?'

Oh, yes, Señor, your Spanish was good, but I thought it would perhaps be easier for you if I gave you directions in English,' she smiled, showing beautiful teeth.

'That's very kind of you, thank you, it would.'

The girl, she was very young, proceeded to explain how to find the address and even drew a little sketch map.

'Thank you very much indeed, you are so kind,' said Paul. 'Muchas gracias, Señorita.'

'My pleasure, Señor,' she smiled.

It was easy to find the Avenida de la Opera using the sketch map, and very soon he was standing in front of Casa de la Musica. There was a brass plate on the wall beside the door, with times of opening. He assumed it was some sort of musical academy.

He went in. It was dark inside and he could not at first see very much. He stood, unsure what to do.

'Señor, permítame ayudarle?' A man had appeared out of the gloom and stood before Paul.

'Oh! Lo siento, sí, estoy buscando Señor Estevan,' said Paul, again surprised how much Spanish he remembered.

'Un momento,' said the man. He turned and disappeared into the darkness.

Why is it so dark? He wondered.

After several minutes the lights were switched on and he could see that he was in a grand vestibule lit by an elaborate chandelier and wall lights. The impressive staircase with carved banisters would have graced any stately home. Paintings hung on the walls. Perhaps not an academy, more like a museum, he thought.

He was surprised again when a different man came up to him.

'Señor? I am Señor Estevan, Sebastian de Castillo Estevan. I understand you are English. I speak English. How can I help you?'

'How do you do, my name is Paul Thomas, I have been asked by a friend, Henry Cartingdon-Bligh, to pick up a parcel from you.'

'Oh, I see, I was expecting Henry to come. Is there something wrong?'

'Henry is not feeling well, I think it was the sea crossing. He is not a good sailor.' He didn't feel it necessary to go into details.

Sebastian laughed. 'Oh, I am sorry, I should not laugh. Please give him my best wishes. I will go and get the item. Please wait here a moment.'

The man had spoken perfect unaccented English and once more Paul wished he could speak better Spanish. But he had made himself understood so perhaps it was not so bad, although they all could tell he was English.

Sebastian came back with a parcel about the size of a box of tissues, neatly wrapped in brown paper and tied with string like parcels used to be fastened before the invention of Sellotape.

'Here is the parcel, please be very careful with it. It is very heavy and very valuable. Tell Henry to take good care of it.' He handed the parcel to Paul with both hands. Paul took it and although he had been warned, he was still surprised at its weight.

'Do not let it out of your sight Señor, please.'

'No, I will be very careful, I assure you.'

'Very well, then I bid you Via con Dios, go with God.' He made a little bow and strode off.

39

Paul was pleased the parcel bore no resemblance to the one in the dream, although it was very heavy. He held it tight, and headed back to the car.

Feeling much better having collected the parcel, he was looking forward to joining his friends. Traffic was light and he was getting used to driving on the wrong side of the road, although it still seemed very strange going anti-clockwise on roundabouts.

On a straight stretch he put his foot down and enjoyed the surge of speed, but then he noticed in his mirror a motorcycle coming up fast behind him. Thinking it might be a policeman about to issue a speeding ticket, he slowed down.

The motorcyclist drew alongside and gestured to him to pull over. He wound down the window.

'Give to me ze package!' the rider demanded in heavily accented English.

The man was clearly not a policeman. Paul put his foot down hard. The improvements that Laura had had done gave the little car performance very much better than when it was new. Even so, he didn't think the car would be able to get away from a motorcycle. He had surprised the rider and had an advantage to begin with. Keeping his foot hard down on the accelerator and keeping one eye on the mirror, he drove the car to its limit. He had never driven the car this fast, and he smiled as he imagined Laura shouting at him to slow down.

The motorbike was gaining again. He couldn't go any faster and there were bends ahead.

A lorry, lumbering along in the middle of the road caused Paul to brake hard and swerve to avoid hitting it. He passed the lorry, narrowly missing an oncoming car whose driver sounded his horn.

He lost sight of the motorbike for a moment and piled on the speed again. Then the motorbike was back, just as fast and gaining on him once more.

Tyres squealing as he took bends far too fast, Paul was panicking. At this rate, he thought, I will kill myself.

Another straight stretch of road opened up and he kept up the speed. The motorbike was with him but not overtaking. If he could keep up this speed maybe he could lose it.

Suddenly, the sound of a siren, urgent and chilling, warned of the approach of an ambulance. A few cars in front of Paul began to pull into the side of the road. The motorbike was still behind. If he slowed down to allow the ambulance to pass, it would catch up.

He could see the ambulance in his mirror, coming very fast, blue light flashing and siren wailing. The motorcyclist was in its path and not pulling over.

Having to slow right down now behind the cars that were pulled over to the side of the road, Paul could see clearly in his mirror. The ambulance

41

clipped the rear of the motorbike causing it to spin, throwing the rider off. The bike spun round on its side in the middle of the road, following cars having to brake hard to avoid it. It all appeared to be happening in slow motion. There was no sign of the rider. He must surely have been badly injured. People were getting out of their cars, no doubt going to investigate the casualty.

For a minute, Paul debated whether he should join them, but the cars in front of him were moving off, so he followed.

Although the biker was clearly not friendly, he felt guilty about the man being injured. He should have stopped. But then, he argued with himself, that might not have been such a good idea. The man wanted to take the parcel with which he was entrusted. He must deliver it safely.

Driving at normal speed, he felt better and tried to enjoy the drive and the scenery.

7

As soon as Paul arrived back at the hotel, he asked Peter if there was any more news of Henry.

'Hello, Paul, where have you been? Why the sudden interest in Henry?'

'I was with him when he was taken ill, then I saw him in the hospital.'

'I didn't know you even knew him.'

'I don't really, met him a few times at club events, that's all.'

'So?'

'He asked me to do an errand for him.'

'Errand?'

'Pick up something for his wife.'

'He hasn't got a wife, he's gay,' Peter said, laughing.

'That's what I thought, but he did say his wife. Anyway, I collected the parcel and I need to give it to him.'

'It will have to wait until he's out of hospital. He's taken a turn for the worse I understand, and can't see anyone. Andrew just told me. In any case he won't be able to give it to his so-called wife in hospital,' Peter laughed again, 'come on, let's see what's happening.'

Still clutching the parcel, Paul went with Peter to join a crowd of men admiring one of the Spanish members' TR3. The bonnet was up, revealing a beautifully detailed engine. All the components and accessories had been polished and it really was a wonderful sight.

'I did that tae the engine of a Roadster I had some years ago, I loved opening it up at garages to see the reaction of the mechanics,' said Gus, dreamily.

The rest of the day was to be taken up with activities centred round the cars, and as Paul was not able to do anything about the parcel, he asked the hotel porter to put it in the safe.

The rally was a great success, everyone enjoyed it immensely. Profuse thanks were offered to the Spanish hosts at the final dinner when trophies were awarded for the various stages.

Henry was still in hospital, so Paul decided to visit him.

'Look, Peter, if I'm not back on time to catch the ferry, don't worry, I have to see Henry,' he explained, when they were assembling ready for departure.

He drove the short distance to the hospital and parked the car, then made his way to Recepción.

He approached the reception desk and asked the young woman, 'Disculpe, estoy preguntando por un amigo mío, el Señor, Henry Cartingdon-Bligh.

'Si, Señor,' The woman consulted a screen and came back a minute later.

'El Señor Henry no está aquí señor, murió en la noche. Lo siento mucho.'

'Dead?' said Paul, shocked.

'Are you English Señor?' asked the young woman.

'Yes, I am, you speak English?'

'Yes, but not well. I am so sorry about your friend. We need to contact his next of kin, is that you?'

'No, no, I'm just a friend, we are members of the same club that's all. I don't know who his next of kin would be.'

'Perhaps I could take your name and address, Señor, as you are the only contact we have. And if you could find out for us who is the next of kin?'

'Yes, of course. Pleased that he still had some of his business cards in his wallet, he offered one to the receptionist. 'Here is my card, I will try to find out for you. Thank you.'

In something of a daze, Paul left the hospital. He had no idea of Henry's relatives; in fact, he knew nothing about the man beyond meeting him on occasions at club meetings. But now he had a parcel belonging to him, a parcel Henry considered valuable. What was he to do? Perhaps if he knew what was in it, he could assess the importance of finding Harry's so-called wife.

Back in the hotel, he took the parcel to his room and looked at it for several minutes before deciding.

He opened his Swiss Army knife and cut through the wrapping. Inside was a plain wooden box with a lid screwed on with eight screws, one at each corner and one in each of the sides. Using the screwdriver attachment on his knife he began to remove the screws. They were hard to budge and the blade slipped several times, risking damaging his fingers.

After several minutes all the screws had been removed and he took off the lid. Inside was another box, metal this time and with no obvious lid. He took it out and turned it over in his hands. There was no way to open it. The box was smooth and featureless. He guessed it must have been welded shut and the welds smoothed over. It was a very well-made box, but why? Whatever is inside must be very valuable, or why go to so much trouble?

He remembered once seeing a silver snuff box with no apparent opening, if you squeezed it in a certain way the lid sprang open, perhaps this was similar - but try as he might, no lid appeared.

He had tried shaking the parcel before he opened it and he shook the box. There was nothing loose inside.

A knock on the door heralded Peter telling him to hurry, they were all ready to leave.

Paul quickly gathered up his things, putting the box in his suitcase, wrapped up in his spare shirt. He left the parcel's wrappings in the waste paper bin.

'OK, Peter, I'm coming!' he shouted.

It had been quite a performance getting all the cars aboard the ship. Too much alcohol over the last few days had affected some of the guys' driving ability. The Spanish sailors had begun to lose their patience.

The next few hours were spent with club members, all relating their experiences over the past few days over more drinks from the ship's bar.

The parcel – now the box, was temporarily removed from Paul's mind.

When they disembarked, Paul drove through the 'Nothing to Declare' lane at customs and was not stopped.

The club members parked near each other and said their noisy farewells before departing on their various ways.

Despite the business with the box, Paul had enjoyed himself immensely. He had not driven well enough to win a trophy but that didn't matter. He had enjoyed renewing his friendship with the club members and he had avoided drinking too much. He realised he was smiling as he drove off in the direction of home.

8

Paul was tired when he returned to Hildisham and all he wanted to do was have a quick shower and sleep.

Next morning, however, almost his first thought was the box that was still wrapped up in his suitcase. He had brought it home because he didn't know what else to do with it. He didn't know who Harry's wife was, if he even had a wife; most of the club guys that knew him thought he was gay. Could he have meant his partner and if so, who was he? Nobody knew. If he had a partner, why did he come to club meetings alone? But then, most of the guys attended club meetings without their spouses.

He took the box from his case and sat looking at it while he ate his breakfast, a rather frugal one as he had forgotten to call at the shop on his way home and there wasn't much in the cupboard or the frig. He really needed to get organised.

'Oh dear,' he thought, 'do I really need another mystery to solve?'

oOo

Several weeks following Paul's return from Spain had been uneventful. He was feeling lonely again but was disinclined to do anything about it. His house was getting very untidy and he hadn't run the hoover round for ages. A pile of junk mail had accumulated on the table by his chair, along with three empty cups and a box that had contained ginger chocolates, bought in Spain. Underneath it all, and forgotten, was the box.

The telephone rang, startling him.

'Yes?'

'Mr Thomas? Paul Thomas?' a woman's voice.

'Yes, how can I help? What are you selling?'

'I am not selling anything, Mr Thomas. You have something of mine. I am Mrs Cartingdon-Bligh – Henry's wife. You have a parcel for me.'

This didn't seem right – he was sure Henry didn't have a wife for one thing, and how had this woman found him?

'Oh, what makes you think that, er Mrs . . .?'

'Cartingdon-Bligh. You left your card with the hospital, remember?'

He did remember, that had been a mistake.

'Well, yes, because I wanted to be informed of Henry's progress, and we had to leave Spain.'

'But you knew Henry had died!'

'Died!' He feigned surprise. 'Oh, I am so sorry.'

'Let's not be foolish, Mr Thomas, we know you knew, and we know you have the parcel.'

'I really don't know what you are talking about. I barely knew your – husband. It was only because he'd been with the car club when he was taken ill that I visited him in hospital. It just seemed a good thing to do. I didn't keep in touch after we returned from Spain so I didn't know he had died. I am really very sorry for your loss. Good bye.' He put the phone down.

Less than a minute later, the phone rang again. He let it ring and when it continued to ring, he put it under a cushion and went into the kitchen.

'Damn woman!' he shouted.

The phone continued to ring – it was not set to go to voicemail – he went out into his tiny garden, but he could still hear the ringing.

In the end he could not stand it any longer, he picked up the phone.

'Yes?'

'You cannot ignore me, Mr Thomas. I want that parcel. And sooner or later, believe me, you will give it to me. Don't delay, Mr Thomas, you won't like the penalty.'

'And I have told you, I know of no parcel. Now leave me alone.' He put down the phone again. It rang again almost immediately.

'How do you switch these things off? He shouted. Throwing the phone across the room, where it continued to ring.

The phone was a remote instrument with a dock for charging; he looked at the dock, wondering how he could disconnect it. The wire led to a point at the wall.

'Aha! Now I've got you!' Unaware that he was talking out loud, he pulled the wire from the socket. The phone stopped ringing. He revelled in the silence, but then realised he had actually been frightened by the menace implied in the phone call. What was the significance of this box? He would have to find out.

Rummaging through the pile of rubbish that had obscured the box, he picked it up. He weighed it in his hands. It was heavy, about three or four pounds he thought, about as much as two bags of sugar. In such a comparatively small box. What could be inside? Gold?

He examined the box closely once more. There was definitely no lid or hinge, nor was there a keyhole. Nothing, just a plain, well finished metal box with rounded corners. It was shiny, but not silver, it looked like stainless steel. It must have been welded shut and then the welds carefully smoothed over. It was going to be difficult to open. He thought for a moment about taking it to his local garage and getting them to cut it open with an oxy-acetylene torch, but quickly dismissed the idea; the contents could be damaged.

He did think for a moment that it might be simpler to just hand it over, but there was obviously something sinister about this box and he was determined to find out what it was. He took it into the garage, where there was a bench and a variety of tools.

He switched on the light over the bench, placed the box in the vice and applied a fine-toothed hacksaw to the shiny surface. The blade just skidded off.

'Damn!' he cursed.

He picked up a large hammer and a hefty chisel. The chisel failed to even scratch the surface and skidded off in the same way the saw had done.

Talking to himself again, he muttered, 'There's got to be a way into it that I'm not seeing.' He took the box out of the vice and examined it closely under the bright light. He looked for any variation in colour that might indicate perhaps a secret opening. He sprayed it with WD40 and left it on the bench. Returning to the kitchen to make coffee and think.

The coffee helped him to think, mainly because it made him sit still for a few minutes.

He tried to remember everything that had led up to collecting the box. Everything that had been said. Why had Henry asked him to pick up the parcel? What had he said about it? What had the people in Torrelavega said? They must have told this woman that he had collected the box.

Try as he might he found it impossible to recall the words of the people he had met in Spain. Finishing his now cold coffee, he returned to the garage.

The WD40 had done the trick. A very faint line had appeared along the side of the box. There was a way in.

In a dusty corner of the garage sat a very old book press, a legacy from Paul's attempt at book-binding. He had purchased the antique press at an auction, but after one or two reasonable efforts, he got tired of all the effort required and he had given up and the press had been pushed away to gather dust.

Now it promised to be the solution to his problem. By fixing a stout bladed knife to the underside of the press and placing the box with the blade on the crack, he thought he would be able to force the box open. The press had a big handle with rounded ends and could be wound down to produce considerable pressure. Gently at first, careful not to displace the blade, he wound the handle down. Then with a bang, the knife pinged out, narrowly missing Paul and clattering across the bonnet of the TR7.

'Blast!' he exclaimed. He picked up the knife and saw that the blade had distorted. He needed something stronger that would withstand the necessary pressure while remaining in place unbent. He remembered his architect's ruler, another auction purchase. The ruler was on his desk in the miniscule study, he ran to fetch it.

The ruler was a heavy wedge of steel with a perfect straight edge, a wonderful tool for drawing or cutting.

Positioning the ruler with its perfect edge along the crack in the box, he was apprehensive. He was afraid that perfect edge might be damaged, but it seemed to be the ideal instrument so he carried on, making sure it was perfectly positioned before beginning to apply pressure.

The heavy handle was difficult to turn once the ruler was in place on the box. Any further downward movement would mean the ruler's edge was being inserted into the box.

He used all his strength to turn the long arms of the handle. There was a fraction of movement, and again, mere millimetres, but it was moving. He hardly dared to look at the box. If the ruler was ejected as the knife had been, it would make a formidable projectile.

A sudden loud crack and the handle spun down. The box fell to the floor and the ruler slid off to the side.

He rushed to pick up the box.

What had been a microscopic line – just a suggestion of a crack that might indicate an opening – was now a definite line, still only a fraction, but an opening.

He was sweating as he placed the box and the ruler in the press again, this time holding the box in place with blocks of wood on either side, held in place with woodworking clamps. He carefully applied pressure. This time everything stayed in place, the handles of the press continued to turn, little by little, the crack widened. More pressure and then, with a loud bang, the box split open.

Paul was jubilant. 'Got you!' he exclaimed.

Quickly releasing the box from its clamps, he carefully took it from the press. The two sides, where there had been no sign of a crack had torn rather than open cleanly. Now it would be possible to lever open the lid and reveal the contents.

He picked up his precious ruler and was relieved to see its edge had not been damaged.

He could hardly contain his excitement as he carried the box to the kitchen and put it on the table.

With a big screwdriver he levered open the lid. The inside of the lid had a thick lining of what looked like lead. That would explain the weight. There was a pad of some sort of compressible material to stop the contents from moving.

There were two rows of little compartments, each one containing what looked like geological or petrological specimens. Closer examination showed small labels alongside each specimen.

He fetched his camera and photographed the open box and then took close-ups of the individual specimens and the labels.

The labels were handwritten and difficult to read, but after some study with the aid of a magnifying glass, Paul came up with a list, which he wrote in his notebook.

Gold Au 56pg
Rhodium Rh 450
Platinum Pt 60
Lutetium Lu (LuCl3) 69
Scandium Sc (Sc2O3) 270
Plutonium Pu 4000
Californium CF (CfBr3) 25mill pg
Francium Fr 1 billion
Lanthanum La

He studied the list of elements and their symbols; he knew a little of the periodic table from school and recognised some of them, but what were the numbers – not atomic weights clearly – could they be values?

Some of the specimens were very tiny and enclosed in sealed glass containers.

He found his well-thumbed copy of the Penguin Dictionary of Science and looked up some of the smallest specimens. The light green coloured speck of Californium, with the symbol in brackets ($CfBr_3$) was evidently Californium Bromide, a radioactive actinide according to the book. The label said 25 mill pg. Surely that could not mean 25 million pounds? But the box came from Spain so perhaps it meant Euros. Could Francium be worth a billion per gram? But the book said no common compounds exist in nature. 'What did that mean? I have some here,' said Paul. 'It's only a tiny brown scrap, but it surely must weigh a gram,' he mused, but he was not familiar with the metric scale, but he did know that it included micrograms, perhaps these were just micrograms of material. Even so, they were evidently valuable. 'Has someone found a way of producing the rare element that was thought not to exist in nature?' he muttered. 'And what of Lanthanum', he wondered, there it is, a tiny scrap of shiny metal, but no details.

Gold and Platinum, they were easy, and the samples were big enough to take out of their little compartments and weigh in his hand, but Paul had not even heard of most of the others. Was this treasure? Could such tiny scraps be worth so much? If they were so valuable it would explain the mysterious caller wanting them back. And it would explain all the mystery in collecting them. The book said that some of them were radioactive – dangerously so, he wondered? Surely such small things could not harm anyone.

He was confused. He sat down and stared at the box, wishing that he had not been involved and most of all wishing that he hadn't opened it.

'Now what am I going to do?' he moaned, sitting at his kitchen table, head in hands. 'Why didn't I simply say, yes, I have the parcel, and just hand it over when someone came to collect it?'

But his inquisitive and suspicious nature had sensed there was more to this than a simple errand, right from the start, and there was the dream, a warning surely.

Henry was gay, or so the club members said, but he could have a wife, gay men, not sure of their sexuality perhaps, do marry women. Or it could be that gay people refer to their partners that way, or do gay men's marriages just have two husbands? Yes, that's right. But the person on the phone, claiming to be his wife, was a woman. Perhaps she really was his wife. The questions went round and round in his head. There were no answers, but he decided, he was right not to have handed it over.

He needed to find someone who knew Henry well. Ideally his actual partner. He had instructed Paul to give the package to his wife. He would ask the guys at the club again if they knew Henry's wife. He had some of the club members' phone numbers - 'that's what I'll do.' He was still talking, or rather muttering, his thoughts out loud.

He picked up the phone and remembered he had pulled out the wire. He spent a few minutes on his knees replacing the plug in the wall socket. He then sat in his armchair and tapped in Peter Warburton's number.

'Peter?'

'Hello, who's this?'

'Peter, it's Paul, from the club . . .'

'Hello!' answered Peter, brightly, 'you OK, I didn't recognise your voice, you sound, I don't know, tired I suppose. What can I do for you?'

'Yes, I am rather. Peter, did you know Henry, the guy at the club?'

'Who died rather tragically?'

'Yes.'

'Why, you didn't know him did you?'

'No, but I need to know about him now.'

'Left it a bit late old man, don't you think?' Peter laughed.

'No, this is serious, Peter. Did you know him or his wife, outside the club, I mean?'

'His wife? I told you he was gay, surely?'

'Yes, but he mentioned his wife to me . . .'

'He must have been having you on. How did that come about?'

'He asked me to collect a parcel that he was going to give to his wife. He couldn't go because he was ill.'

'Oh, I see, so did you?'

'I collected the parcel, and I have it here, but I don't know what to do with it.'

'That is a puzzle. Tell you what, I'll ask a few of the guys. We're having a bit of a recap of the rally on Saturday. You should have had an invite. It's at the usual place. You could ask them yourself.'

'I haven't had anything. It's not just for committee members then?'

'No, everyone is welcome. Did you take any photos, bring them if you did. Shall I see you there then?'

'Yes, OK, Peter, thanks, bye now.'

'Take care! Bye.'

Paul put down the phone.

Did he want to have to explain to people at the club about the box? He could not ask about Henry

61

without explaining. Was that a good idea? Probably not.

Looking at the list of contents again, he wondered about the values of the specimens. It was easy to find the price of gold, it would be on the internet, but the rarer ones, he wasn't sure.

He thought of Johnson Matthey, the refiners in Royston and wondered if he could find out from them. He could ring them himself but he didn't want to admit to having the specimens.

9

Still thinking of Johnson Matthey, it sudden occurred to Paul that the reason he knew of the refiners was from when he lived in Cambridgeshire, not far from where the firm was based, in Royston, just across the border in Hertfordshire, and that led him to think of his old friend, Clive, who still lived in Cambridgeshire, quite near to Royston in fact – maybe he knows someone who works there. 'That's it!' he shouted, 'I'll ask him.'

Somewhere among all his notebooks and diaries, would be Clive's number.

He's sure to still be there I'm sure, he thought as he leafed through page after page of scribbled notes. Clive lived in a large village in Cambridgeshire, just over the county border From Royston. The refiners employed people from a wide radius. Clive knew a lot of people; he was sure to know someone.

'Ah! Here it is! I knew I had it. Just hope he hasn't moved.

He tapped in the number.

'Hello?'

'Clive?'

'Yes.'

'It's Paul, Paul Thomas, remember me? It's a long time ago.'

'Paul! Good grief, of course I remember you. How are you. Gosh, fancy hearing from you. How are you?'

'I'm OK, Thanks. How are you?'

'Oh, you know, advancing years and all that, but, tell me, why the call after all this time, not that I'm complaining, it really is good to hear from you.'

'Yes, it's a bit cheeky, Clive, but I want a favour.'

'So, tell me. I'll be happy to help if I can.'

'Do you know anyone that works at Johnson Matthey's?'

'Lots of people round here work there, sure I know people, why?'

'I need some information, but I can't just ask openly because that would give away that I have something certain people want.'

'Gosh, cloak and dagger stuff, what are you into, Paul. It sounds dodgy.'

'It could be, but not for you. I just need to know about some precious metals.'

'You can find everything on the internet you know.'

'Yes, of course, but if I ask on the web, someone might be watching my computer. But if a third party, who is nothing to do with me, were to make enquiries, it would not flag up interest – do you see?'

'I think so. I'll see what I can do, Paul. What are these precious metals?'

'I can't risk telling you about them over the phone and I can't email anything about them or anything like that.' He paused, 'Can I come over and see you?'

'That would be great! We'll have a lot of catching up to do. When do you want to come? We have sofa bed you could sleep on.'

'I could leave in a few minutes and be with you, what, midday?'

'You remember where I live?'

'Of course, how could I forget those late-night home-made wine sessions!'

Not intending to stay long with his friend, Paul checked everything was switched off, stuffed the box, carefully wrapped in a tee shirt along with a minimum of clothing and a wash-kit into a bag and threw it into the car.

For a moment he thought of the times he would have had to ask his neighbours to look after Mr. Brown, his lovely old tabby cat when he went away, but since the animal had died, he couldn't bring himself to have another cat.

Paul guessed it was about sixty miles to Clive's place, and on lightly trafficked roads he should be there in about ninety minutes.

It was a fine sunny day, so the hood of the TR came down. 'That's better,' he said to himself, sliding into the leather seat.

Clive was waiting for Paul as he drove into the yard, which was surrounded by large barns.

Clive and his father had been hay and straw merchants but Clive gave up the business when his father died. He had begun dealing in antiques and no doubt the barns would have been useful to store goods. But there was no sign saying 'Antiques', had he given that up as well?

'Hello, old chum, my goodness, the years haven't been kind to you', quipped Clive, greeting Paul with an enthusiastic handshake. 'Nice car! What is it?'

'No, you old bugger, they haven't. How have they been treating you?'

'I've got something to show you!' said Clive, not bothering to answer, but indicating that Paul should follow him.

He headed for one of the barns and pulled open the big double doors.

Inside were two enormous shiny traction engines. Clive beamed. 'What do you think? Castor and Pollux, and there are more – come on.' He headed to another barn and opened the doors. Two more beautiful big engines. 'I call these two, Romulus and Remus,' said Clive, with a big grin.

Clive had not given Paul chance to respond, but now he stood, waiting for him to speak.

'They're amazing! I knew you were interested in steam engines of course, the working engines your dad used to use way back, but these are wonderful.'

'We can get one steamed up if you like, but of course, you like cars don't you, come this way.'

Paul followed Clive, who was almost dancing with excitement showing his treasures.

Another barn, not as high but wider, had several doors which Clive proceeded to open.

'What do you think of those?'

Inside the dimly lit barn, Paul could see rows of old cars, some covered with dust sheets. There were Jaguars, Aston Martins, Austins, a bright red Dennis fire engine and many more. He was almost speechless, he had to consciously close his mouth which had fallen open.

'I've been wanting to show them off to someone who didn't know them. The collection belonged to a friend. I bought the whole lot from his wife when he died. Aren't they wonderful? Go in, have a good look round, take your time,' urged Clive, still beaming.

'There's nothing I would like better, Clive, but I have something I have to do urgently right now. Perhaps I could come another time . . .' He could see the disappointment on his friend's face, and felt bad.

'Yes, of course, I understand, but you do like them?'

'Course I do, I love them, and I would love to see an engine steaming, but as I say, I am rather pressed just now.'

'Come in the house then, cup of coffee?' Clive was trying hard to stay cheerful as he led Paul into his kitchen, where Jacqui, Clive's wife was preparing food for her many animals and birds.

'Hello, Paul, goodness, it's been a long time, where have you been hiding?'

'Not hiding exactly, my job took me all over the shop. I'm retired now and I can catch up with old friends.'

'Well, now you've remembered us, keep in touch, OK?' Smiling, she left the kitchen with bowls of animal feed.

Over coffee, Paul tried to explain his situation without giving too much away. Clive listened, looking uneasy.

'So, If I can get someone to value these – metals, then what?'

'That's it as far as you need to know, I don't really know myself what to do next.'

'Tell me, how did you get these, what did you call them, specimens?'

'I really can't tell you now. It's a long story. When it's all over, then perhaps I could come and see you again and I'll tell you all about it.'

'OK, it's a deal. I do know someone who should be able to help, and I think I can count on him to be discrete.'

'That is essential.'

'Do you want to meet the guy then, or shall I just give him your list?'

'I do need to speak to him.'

'Give me a sec. I'll phone him, get him to come round. He lives in the village.'

While they waited for Clive's friend to come, the two men exchanged stories of what they had been doing in the many years since Paul had lived in the area.

Jacqui brought in a huge bird which she said was an eagle owl. 'Hold out your arm,' she said, and the bird hopped onto Paul's arm. It looked at him with huge orange eyes.

'My goodness, does it want to eat me?' exclaimed Paul. 'I've never seen such an enormous bird. It's magnificent.'

They all laughed and Paul was pleased to have had his mind taken off the box for a few moments.

Tim Brookes, who worked as a metallurgist in the refining company was the ideal person to help Paul. He claimed to know all there was to know about precious metals, their uses and perhaps what's more, their values.

'And you have all these?' he said, when Paul showed him the list.

'Yes, only tiny specimens, but yes.'

'Californium is only dealt with in micrograms. A gram of it would be unheard of and even a tiny amount would be worth an astronomic figure. And you say you have some Francium? I've never even seen any. What colour is it?'

'It's encased in glass, it's a sort of brownish . . .'

'Yes, of course, it will be lead glass, it's highly radioactive, but the glass should help. Don't touch any of them will you. Several are radioactive. Although I am familiar with these materials – theoretically at least, I don't actually get to see them. They are so rare. Even if your samples are very tiny, they will be worth a great deal of money – to the right people.'

'Can you be more specific?' Paul asked.

'Let's look at the list again, well gold and platinum – I deal with those all the time so that's easy, Rhodium, yes, but the others, well, as I said I hardly ever see most of them. I can guesstimate values. I mean, I'd love to see them. It's anybody's

70

guess, really.' He sat staring at the list and making humming noises. 'I can't give you an accurate figure of course because I don't know the weights and to be honest, I don't know anything about some of them. Just to give you an idea, I would say, certainly more than a million. That's the best I can do. Is there any chance I could see them?'

'No, I'm sorry, they are locked up very securely and I daren't let anyone see them. There are some people who want them very much, and until I can find out more, they're staying out of sight. I must ask you not to mention any of this to anyone. Do you understand? But can you tell me why they are so valuable?'

'Mainly their rarity. They do have uses in research and some are used in cancer detection and treatment. Some rare metals are used in electronics. I'm afraid it is all more than I am qualified to comment on.'

'Well, thank you, Tim, you have been helpful. Not a word, OK?'

Tim agreed, but pleaded to be told, when it was possible, more about the specimens. Paul agreed.

'Right then, nice to meet you, Paul. See you down the pub, Clive?' said Tim as he left.

'Was that a help?' asked Clive.

'Yes, he confirmed that these specimens are very valuable and very rare, and possibly dangerous. I wish I had never seen them,' said Paul ruefully.

'What are you going to do?'

'Right now? Do you fancy a pint?'

10

Paul remembered The Hoops, Clive's local, but it had changed since he lived in the village, thirty or more years ago. They settled at a table where they could watch people.

'Why do you think there is dirty work and such involved, Paul?' Clive asked, after bringing two pints of Doom Bar to the table.

'Simply because they, whoever they are, keep insisting I hand over the box. They don't say anything about what's inside. They threatened me with dire consequences if I don't hand it over. Also, the way I was asked to pick up the box and bring it back to the UK. It was all very mysterious. And the guy that asked me to pick it up died while we were in Spain. He had only drunk too much, nothing serious, next thing he's dead.'

'Was he a friend?' Clive asked.

'No, I hardly knew him at all, I'd bumped into him at car club meetings, that's all. Then, when he had drunk himself silly, I helped some of the other guys to get him to his room.'

'So why did he ask you to pick up the parcel?'

'That's the question, why me?'

'Didn't you think it strange at the time?'

'I suppose it was because I was there, having helped him to his room, the others had gone, I was the last to leave, he called me back. It was only later I thought it a bit strange.'

'Mm,' mumbled Clive. 'I have heard of people being asked to take contraband and such through customs having been given all sorts of reasons why the owner couldn't take it themselves. This sounds like the same thing to me. So how did you get it through customs?'

'I didn't give it a thought – just drove through the nothing to declare channel. I wasn't stopped.'

'That was lucky. If you'd been caught with all that stuff you'd have been in trouble.'

'But there was no way of knowing what was in the box.'

'There was if it was radioactive!' laughed Clive.

'Oh, yes, I hadn't thought of that.'

'So, if Tim can find out about these rare elements, what are you going to do?' Clive asked.

'I have absolutely no idea. I don't want to just hand them over to these people because I'm sure they are crooks of some kind. I could go to the police, but I'm not a popular person with them . . .'

'Oh! Tell me more,' said Clive, eagerly.

'It's just that, in the course of my work I have fallen foul of them a few times, nothing serious – really.'

'Are you sure? Tell me about them.'

'Not now, Clive. If I write my memoirs, you can read all about my problems with the police. But right now, I have a more pressing problem.'

'Another?' asked Clive, waving his glass, his response to most problems.

'I'll get them, it might help the grey cells to come up with something.'

Paul was surprised at the price of beer in Cambridgeshire. It was another reason to cut back on alcohol.

'I'm trying to cut down, Clive, I'll just have this one more, OK?' said Paul as he brought the two fresh pints from the bar and handed one to his friend.

'Oh, that's a shame, why's that?'

'I can't go into it now, if you don't mind. OK?'

'Of course, so what do you drink instead?'

'Coffee mainly. So far it's not too bad.'

After a few minutes of silence, no doubt imagining life without beer, Clive asked, 'I'd love to see these minerals, Paul, won't you show them to me?'

'What?' said Paul, waking from his reverie. 'Well, I suppose it wouldn't hurt. We'll go back to yours and I'll show them to you when we're completely alone.'

'Jacqui might be there,' said Clive.

'I'm sure I can trust Jacqui to keep shtum,' said Paul.

Paul sat for a moment then leaned forward, as if to whisper. 'Clive, you'll think I'm barmy, but – well, I had a dream, and . . .'

'A dream?'

'Yes, and it seemed as if it was some sort of warning, oh, no, I can't tell you, it's silly.'

'Go on, I won't think it's silly if you think it's important. Tell me.'

'In this dream, I'm asked to pick up a parcel from an address that sounded very much like the address I was asked to go to – at the time it seemed like an allegory of my life, but then when things seemed to pan out in real life – oh, I don't know. Do you think I am going doolally?'

'That is strange – like a premonition you mean. What happened in the dream? What did you do with the box?'

'That's the problem, the dream ended before I had disposed of the box.'

They returned to Clive's house without saying much. Even Clive seemed to have run out of stories. Jacqui was out. Clive was keen to see the box.

'Your dream does sound like some sort of warning, doesn't it? Come on, Paul, show it to me,'

Paul opened his overnight bag and unwrapped the box from a tee shirt. He held it out for Clive to see. 'I had to damage it to get it open.' He opened the lid. Clive leaned forward to see.

'Don't get too close, some of the samples are radioactive. I don't know if they are dangerous.'

'Gosh, and those little bits could be worth a million?' Clive breathed.

'Evidently.'

'Gosh,' said Clive again.

'Have you got anywhere we could hide it, Clive? It isn't safe in my bag.'

'Not really, I never needed a safe. But, wait a minute, what if we put it in a secret compartment in a piece of antique furniture?'

'Do you still do antiques then?'

'No, I gave it up, too much like hard work and not enough reward, but I do still have one or two pieces. I've got a very nice eighteenth-century desk bureau with drawers. It has several secret hiding places that would be suitable. Nobody could guess they are there.'

'Show me,' said Paul.

Paul thought the piece of furniture was beautiful, and was intrigued when Clive showed him the secret compartments, hidden behind drawers. He agreed that nobody could guess they were there.

'That's it then, we'll stow the box in there, for now anyway.'

After Clive had closed up the bureau, Paul felt calmer than he had for a while.

Clive suggested Paul stay for a while and try to forget the box and its troubles. He was keen to show off his collection and to get an engine steaming. He knew Paul liked steam railway engines and wanted to get him interested in traction engines.

'Have you ever driven a traction engine, Paul?' Clive asked as they browsed among the historic vehicles in the larger of his barns.

'No, I must admit I haven't really taken a great deal of interest in them, apart from admiring photographs on the internet and knowing a little about their use in farming. I did once have a ride on the footplate of a little railway engine at Didcot when a friend who knew people there took me. That was exciting, but of course I didn't handle the controls.'

'Of course you know we used them when my dad was alive', began Clive, 'and although working with them was an everyday thing, I loved them right from when I was a little boy. It has become a passion now, an obsession even, and although I can't really afford it, I keep adding them to my collection whenever possible. Come on, I'll show you how to get one steamed up.'

Paul watched as Clive worked on a very fine engine that had been painstakingly restored and was now a beautiful example of past engineering. He could see the appeal of course, but it was railway engines that got his pulse racing.

It was a long process getting the engine ready and Paul was beginning to think about a cup of tea or a pint of beer rather than sitting on a smelly engine.

'All ready, climb up, Paul', called Clive at last, 'we'll just take her round the yard, just to let you get the hang of it,' Clive had to shout over the noise of the machinery.

The next hour was a revelation to Paul. The smell of hot oil and steam was the same as that of a railway engine, and being up close to all the machinery was exciting. He had a huge grin on his face as he wound the big steering wheel and trundled the heavy engine round and round the yard.

'Enjoying it?' asked Clive, also grinning.

'It's great fun, I never realised. All this power is intoxicating. No wonder you like them so much.'

11

When Clive was able to tear Paul away from the engine, they returned to the house where Jacqui had just come back from feeding her animals.

'Don't say we've got another steam fanatic to deal with!' Jacqui quipped as she watched Paul washing his hands at the kitchen sink.

'Looks like it, never seen anyone with a bigger grin on his face,' said Clive, laughing. 'Coffee?'

'Oh, yes please, that would be nice,' said Paul, 'I've worked up quite a thirst.'

'Would you mind, Jacqui? Only we have things to discuss – we'll be in the sitting room.'

'Just this once, then, as we have a guest,' said Jacqui.

The two men sat in the comfortable chairs in the sitting room and Clive was about to speak, when he noticed the bureau had been moved.

'Jacqui!' he called. 'Where have you moved the bureau to?'

'That old one, you mean?' came the reply.

'Yes, of course.'

'Sold it!' came the reply.

'What! Come in here.'

'Why, wasn't it for sale?' said Jacqui as she came in with mugs of coffee, 'I got a good price for it. It's been kicking about for ages, I thought you wanted to sell it.'

'Well, I did, but I changed my mind. I wanted to keep it. Who did you sell it to?'

'Chap came round this afternoon while you were playing with steam engines, wanting to know if you were still dealing. I told him most of the stuff had gone. He spotted the bureau and said he would like it if the price was right.'

'And was it? what did he give you for it?'

'Fifteen hundred – cash!'

Turning to Paul, who was now looking extremely anxious, Clive asked, 'Now what are we going to do?' Then, to Jacqui, 'Did you get his name and address?'

'I've got his card – where did I put it?'

After a lot of searching though pockets, Jacqui came up with the card, which read:

Anton Sveringe, dealer in fine art and antiques.
44 Clifton Road, Clifton Industrial Estate. Cambridge.
CG1 7ED Telephone: 01223 949743
e-mail sveringe@yahoo.com

'It looks genuine, at least. I'll give him a ring,' said Clive, taking the card.

'What are you going to say?' asked Paul.

'Just tell him it wasn't for sale, and to bring it back.'

'What if he won't?'

'He'll have to, surely,' said Clive, uncertainly, 'won't he?'

'Not if he thinks he's got a bargain, which he has, whichever way you look at it.'

'I'm sorry, Paul. Oh dear! I can but try.'

'He won't find the hidden drawer though, will he?'

'He might, if he's a dealer!'

'Never mind phoning, we've got to find him!' said Paul. 'How are you for time, Clive, do you fancy a trip to Cambridge?'

'Yes, of course.'

'Now?'

'Yes, let's go.'

'Do you mind if I have a go in your car, Paul?'

Paul was always reluctant to let anyone drive the TR. He could hear his wife saying, 'It's only insured for me,' but he couldn't refuse his good friend. 'Of course, here,' he threw the keys to Clive, who was already making for the driver's side of the car.

It doesn't take long to get to Cambridge from Clive's house, but finding the industrial estate took a little longer.

'Haven't you got satnav?' asked Clive after they had driven round some time trying to follow the directions given by a helpful man they had asked.

'I had in the firm's car, but no, never needed it – well not until now.' He laughed.

'Oh, look, here we are!' exclaimed Clive, pointing to a large sign which read, Clifton Industrial Estate. 'And it's got a list of firms, too.'

They were able to find Sveringe Antiques easily, using the plan.

'Here goes,' said Clive, getting out of the car.

He approached the reception desk and asked for Mr Sveringe.

'Who shall I say?'

'Just say a customer.'

'Just a moment.' The young woman spoke into an intercom device, 'Mr Sveringe? Customer for you, at the front desk.'

Mr Sveringe was just what Clive expected, short dark, bearded and bespectacled, and wearing a dark suit with a fancy, gold embroidered waistcoat. He spoke with a middle European accent.

'Yes sir, is there a specific item you are interested in?'

'Well yes, you bought an eighteenth-century desk bureau recently. I would like to buy it.'

'How did you know? It doesn't matter anyway; it is sold already. I'm sorry. We have others you may like.'

'Who did you sell it to?' Clive asked.

'I can't tell you that – only that it is being shipped to the Netherlands.'

'When?'

'Today, as it happens. I'm sorry, I can't help you with that piece.'

'Can you at least tell me which port it is being shipped from?' Clive persisted.

'Not that is any concern of yours, as I have said, because it is sold. But it will go from Harwich. Now, please sir, I cannot help you. You have missed the boat – literally!' he laughed and turned away, walking briskly from whence he came.

Clive thanked the receptionist and returned to the car.

'Any luck?' Paul asked, anxiously.

'No, he's already sold it on, and it's going to Rotterdam today!'

'My God! Rotterdam! Where from? Did you get a name?'

'Going from Harwich, and no, he wouldn't tell me the name of his customer. What are we going to do?'

'We have to get to Harwich and either stop it going or get the box somehow.'

'Oh dear!' said Clive.

'Are you still with me? Because if not I'll understand, but I have to get there as soon as possible. If you are with me, we can go now.'

'Yes, of course I'm with you; do you know the way to Harwich?'

'Well, not from here, but I think I will find it. Via Bury, I should think, I know the way from there.'

Just under two hours later they found themselves in the bewildering port complex of Harwich and had to ask where they might find a ship headed for Holland.

'There she is look!' almost shouted Clive as he spotted the funnel of a ship sticking out over some buildings.

The ship, the MV Maria, it had to be the one, mused Paul, as the only ship they could see was stilling loading cargo. Paul approached one of the men loading a large crate onto a crane.

'Excuse me, can you tell me if you have loaded an antique desk?'

'Don't know, mate, I just loads 'em, I don't ask how old they are, but if it's going it's already loaded, this is the last one. Ship sails at midnight.'

'Can I get aboard?'

'Don't ask me, mate, strictly shoreside me, I get sea-sick.'

'OK, thanks a lot.'

Paul turned to Clive, who was standing behind him.

'It's already on board. We obviously can't get the desk back, but if we can get on board, we might find it and get the box. What do you think?'

'Did he say the ship sails at midnight?'

'Yes.'

'It'll be dark well before that – if we could sneak aboard . . .'

'Good thinking. We have to try. Come on, lets come back later then.'

Clive appeared to be enjoying the situation, but Paul was increasingly worried. What if they were unable to retrieve the box. The people who wanted it would not believe what had happened to it.

12

It was quiet and dark when the two men returned to the dockside where the ship lay, all ready to sail at midnight. There appeared to be no-one about. Perhaps the crew have gone ashore for a night out before their voyage, Paul suggested.

'What's the plan?' Clive asked.

'No plan, we just go aboard as if we have a right to. Come on, don't rush, just take it slowly.'

Clive found it difficult to act innocently, but tried to follow Paul's example as he climbed the gangway up to the deck.

'Find the way into the hold,' whispered Paul.

They walked round the superstructure looking for a way in. Paul stopped and pointed to a door with the legend, "Hold 1" painted on it.

'Here we go.'

The door was open and led to a flight of metal steps which were dimly lit by a bulkhead lamp. Another door at the bottom opened into the hold.

'It said "Hold 1" on the door, so there's more than one. Let's hope this is the one we need,' said Paul, shining his torch around the stacks of boxes and crates.

'How are we going to find it in all this lot?' asked Clive, who was now feeling very nervous.

'Just keep looking,' urged Paul.

The boxes were arranged in stacks with spaces between, so searching was easy. Most of the boxes had their contents and destinations listed on paper labels stapled to them, but one item was not in a box, but appeared to be wrapped in many layers of bubble wrap. It's label simply read 'Sveringe' Rotterdam.

'This is it!' exclaimed Clive as he bent to read the label. 'Have you got a knife?'

Paul began to attack the packing with his Swiss Army knife and soon revealed the gleaming mahogany surface of the desk. He turned to smile at Clive, who was holding the torch.

'Just cut away the bit near the drawer, we should be able to get at the hidden compartment without uncovering too much.'

It took a few minutes, but Paul was soon able to slide out the drawer, behind which was the hidden compartment containing the box.

'Got it!' Paul whispered, 'Let's go!'

They were almost at the gangplank and escape, when a shout came from somewhere, 'Stop! Who are you?'

A large bearded man in uniform appeared in front of them, blocking their exit. He repeated his question in a thick Dutch accent.

'What are you doing aboard my ship? Who are you? Are you trying to stow away? I will call the police.' He didn't wait for a reply and when Paul and Clive tried to barge past him, he was too quick and grabbed them both and pushed them face first against the superstructure.

'Eric, kom hier snel, ik heb gevangenen!' he shouted.

Paul and Clive struggled but could not break free from the man's grip, on each of their arms. They guessed he had called for help. They would just have to try and explain.

'Wat is het, schipper? Wie zijn deze jongens?' asked another uniformed man who appeared as suddenly as had the first man.

'Ik betrapte ze erop dat ze probeerden weg te komen. Neem ze mee naar beneden en sluit ze op, de politie bellen,' said the captain.

Although neither man understood Dutch, it was clear what had been said. They were to be locked up until the police came.

'Oh dear, here we go again,' said Paul, as they were manhandled into a small room somewhere in the depths of the ship.

'What do you mean, again?'

'I told you, I've had a few run-ins with the police, never a pleasant experience. They never seem to accept my explanations.'

Clive was wondering what he'd let himself in for by agreeing to help Paul. He sat with his head in his hands and said no more.

They waited what seemed to be a long time until noises of considerable activity made them wonder what was going to happen to them. If the ship sailed on time, before the police arrived, would the two men be unwitting passengers?

Then, at almost midnight, with the ship's engines warming up and the two men getting more and more anxious, the door opened and two uniformed policemen gestured for them to come out.

'On your feet, come on, or you will be pressganged!' quipped one of the policemen.

They were quickly bundled off the ship, and in to a waiting police car.

'We'll get you to the station and then you can tell us all about it,' said the other policemen.

Harwich Police Station looks like a big house from the outside, but is totally undomestic in appearance inside.

'Wait in here. I'll get the inspector,' said the constable, as they were ushered into a waiting room. 'He won't be long.'

'Have you still got the box?' asked Clive, after a while.

'Yes, as soon as that big guy appeared I shoved in my pocket.'

'What are we going to say?' asked Clive, anxiously.

'I'll just tell the truth,' Paul answered, with more confidence than he felt.

'Will they believe us?'

'Probably not, they don't usually believe me. Mind, I've never dealt with Essex Police before, they may be different.'

'But you don't think they will?'

'No.'

They sat in silence for the next twenty minutes or so. Clive was probably wishing he had never set eyes on Paul, while Paul was wishing he hadn't got his friend into this mess.

The door opened and both men looked up, anxiously.

'Gentlemen,' announced the incomer, with an unpleasant smile on his face. 'Aren't you two a bit old to be stowing away?'

'We weren't stowing away . . .' began Paul.

'No, I don't think you were, it's more serious than that isn't it? Do you want to tell me all about it?'

'It's a long story,' said Paul, and Clive nodded.

'Aren't they all?' said the policeman. 'My name is Inspector Radcliffe, Essex CID, and this, he turned as another man entered the room, 'is DS Brooks, also of the Essex CID. Keep up, man. Now tell me who you are.'

The two detectives sat on one side of the table and the two adventurers on the other. They sat looking at each other for an uncomfortable minute. All part of their technique, guessed Paul.

'My name is Paul Thomas, I live in Hildisham, and this is my friend Clive Flack and he lives in Cambridgeshire.'

'Thank you. Hildisham, that's Norfolk isn't it? Have you got that Sergeant? Right, now we know who we all are, tell me what you were doing on board a foreign vessel in the middle of the night?'

Paul nodded to Clive. 'Clive is an antique dealer and his wife sold a valuable antique desk without Clive's knowledge or permission. We were hoping to get it back.'

'You mean you were hoping to steal it.'

'Not exactly, you see it was not meant for sale.'

'But it was sold, you said so, if you were trying to get it back, and it was no longer your property, you were trying to steal it.'

'Yes, but.'

'There's no but about it. How did you think you might get it off the ship? I guess a desk would be quite large and heavy.'

'Well, yes, we hadn't got that far.'

'No, you are pretty useless thieves in fact.'

'You could say that, because we aren't really thieves . . .'

'Only because you were caught before you actually stole anything. You intended to steal the item of furniture.' The inspector looked hard at Paul and then at Clive. 'Now, do you want to tell me the real story. I enjoyed the fairy-tale, but it didn't wash.'

'But it's true, Inspector.'

'So, how did you plan to get it off the boat?'

'We hadn't thought it through . . .' muttered Paul.

'You certainly hadn't thought it through, and now you are charged with trespass and attempted stowing away. Not to mention conspiring to commit the theft of a valuable piece of antique furniture.'

'We haven't been charged with anything – so far,' offered Clive.

'Oh, take them away, Brooks, we'll talk to them again later. Perhaps they will tell us the real story when they've had time to think.'

Locked in a waiting room again, the two friends were trying to think what they could tell the inspector.

'At least we aren't in a cell,' said Clive.

'No, that comes later, after they charge us. And charge us they will if we can't satisfy them that we were not doing anything illegal.'

'Why don't we tell them exactly what we were doing – retrieving your geological specimens. They can't know they are valuable,' said Clive.

'No, they can't can they, good thinking, my friend. That's what we'll do. Shall I call them, or wait until they fetch us?'

'Call them!'

They were sat round the table once more.

'I take it you have decided to tell us the truth at last,' said the inspector.

'We were trying to get my little collection of geological specimens. They were in a drawer in the desk.'

'And did you find them?'

'Yes.'

'Let me see.'

Paul took out the box and put it on the table.

'Open it,' said the policeman.

Paul opened the box.

The inspector peered at the specimens. 'Are they valuable?'

'Only to me,' said Paul.

The inspector was looking closely and reading the labels. 'You've gold I see, and a lot of stuff I've never heard of.'

'There's only the tiniest bit of gold, and all the other specimens are very small. No value except to a geologist or petrologist.'

'What's a petrologist?'

'One who studies rocks,' said Paul.

'Why are they in such a strong box. Are you sure they aren't valuable?'

'It was just a convenient box to put them in that's all.'

'Mm. What do you think, Brooks. Do you know anything about – petrology?'

'Sorry, sir, no. I used to collect pebbles from the seaside and tumble them in a machine to polish them, they looked lovely, all shiny and different colours . . .'

'Yes, yes, I'm sure, we don't want to hear about your pebbles, Sergeant!'

'Sorry, Sir.'

'What do you think about these two? Do you think this latest story is the truth? Oh, wait a minute,' he turned to Clive. 'What's your involvement in this?'

'It was my bureau.'

'So why were Mr Thomas's bits of rock in your bureau?'

'He just put them in there while he was staying with us.'

'I see, I think.'

'We didn't do any harm, Inspector,' Paul pleaded.

'No, no, I don't think you did, other than wasting police time.' He looked hard at the two unfortunate adventurers and then at the sergeant. After a moment's thought he stood up. 'All right, you can go. See them out, Brooks.'

'I suppose it would be too much to ask for a lift back to the car,' mused Clive when they were outside.

'Yes, I think so. It isn't far.'

13

'Are the police always like that?' asked Clive when at last they got back to the car.

'They were pussycats compared to most I've had to deal with. At least they let us go. I began to wonder.'

'What are we going to do now?' asked Clive.

'Did you say, 'we?' are you including yourself in my problem?'

'I already nearly got locked up by being with you, so I guess the answer is yes. I want to help in any way I can.'

'That's good to know, Clive, but this thing could lead into all sorts of trouble, I don't know that I can risk involving you.'

'I think I've already demonstrated my willingness to risk danger and such, Paul. I'm with you, OK.'

Paul was quite overcome by his friend's loyalty, he couldn't speak, just held out his hand for Clive to shake.

After a minute or two, Paul asked Clive if he had any ideas.

'Let's think about it. You have the box, but you don't know who it was meant for, right? And we know that some people want to get hold of it, right? The police are no help . . .'

'Nothing new there!' Paul interrupted.

'No, so who can we ask, who might know Harry's so-called wife?'

'You're right about all that. The only people who may know Harry's wife – we have to call her that as we have nothing else to go on – are the guys at the car club. I did ask some of them but they didn't know. Others may, so that has to be our next step. Talk to the guys from the club. Trouble is, I don't know where they live.'

'Do you have the secretary's address?'

'I have an e-mail for the club, I suppose that must be the secretary's contact address,' said Paul.

'That's what we do, email him and ask to meet.'

'Well don!' said Paul, slapping Clive on the back. 'You aren't just a pretty face, are you? Come to think of it, you aren't that either! But you have brains, and that's better.' Paul laughed, he felt better, and was grateful he had Clive on his side.

'Right then, back to mine,' said Paul.

'Can I drive, Paul?' Clive asked

Paul only hesitated for a moment, 'Yes, of course,' he said, getting out of the car and going round to the passenger side. 'Be careful with her. It w–'

'I do know, Paul,' said Clive, interrupting, 'you told me before,' Clive smiled as he slid into the driver's seat. 'I'll be careful.'

Clive was careful, and Paul was happy to let him drive all the way back to Hildisham.

Clive, who seemed to know the road, reckoned it was about a hundred miles to Hildisham and driving 'carefully' it would take a couple of hours. Paul for once a comfortable passenger, sat back and listened to his friend's stories.

Clive is an excellent raconteur and can talk endlessly about steam engines and farming and anything else you care to mention. The hour and a half flew by.

It was nearly dark when they arrived at Fishers' Lane and Clive parked the TR on the drive.

'I'll get some coffee on, and then we can either go down to the front and get fish and chips, or I could rustle up an omelette or something. What do you say?' said Paul, climbing out to the car.

'Me finks fish and chips sounds very good, we'll do that,' said Clive. 'Do we walk down?'

Paul was ahead of Clive, opening the front door of the cottage, 'Oh! Oh my God! Look at this! We've been burgled!' Paul was shouting as he saw more and more evidence of a break-in. Clive was behind him and was horrified to see the damage that had been done. Furniture had been turned over, books removed from the bookcase, just left in heaps on the floor. Clive, who knew about such things, could see that some of them, leather bound volumes, were valuable. He bent to pick up an early copy of Johnson's Dictionary, putting it carefully on the bookcase.

Paul was examining his precious portrait of Laura that hung over the fireplace. The portrait had been painted by a local artist soon after they were married and it was a remarkable likeness.

'Thank God they haven't damaged this,' he said, adjusting it slightly. 'Best not touch anything, Clive, until the police have seen it. How did they know I live here?' he said, ignoring his own advice, picking up a broken chair.

'You think it's the people after the box?'

'Of course, it has to be.'

'Here, let me help,' said Clive, picking up more upended furniture. 'Actually, it isn't all that bad when you look closely, they haven't actually broken much.' But Paul was not listening, he was in his little study.

'Come and look at this! Not done much damage you say, look at this!' He gestured at the debris on the desk and floor. 'The printer has been smashed, and where's my laptop? Oh God, I hope they haven't taken that.'

Clive was on his knees gathering up piles of paper from the floor. 'No, it's here, look, under the desk. It has printing ink all over it but I don't think it's broken.'

'Phew! That's a relief, the other stuff doesn't really matter, but everything is on that laptop, priceless stuff – all about my adventures, you know, the makings of a book perhaps.'

'Haven't you got it backed up?' Clive asked incredulously.

'Backed up – how do you mean?'

'I keep my documents and such on memory sticks. Then if the computer fails, I still have the files.'

Paul nodded, but was not really listening. He was wondering how the burglars had got his address.

'I'll get the coffee on, shall I?' asked Clive.

'What? Oh, yes, thanks, I'll just tidy up a bit . . .'

'What about the police?'

'No, I don't think I'll bother them after all. Not much they can do anyway.'

Sitting in the living room, restored to something resembling order by Clive, the two men drank their coffee in silence. While looking for coffee, Clive had found Paul's hidden bottle of Jamieson's and had added generous slugs to the coffee.

'I don't like this at all, you know,' said Paul at last.

'Oh, sorry, I thought a drop of whiskey would help.'

'No, no, not the whiskey, of course, no, this whole business. I vowed I wouldn't get into any more scrapes when I retired, and here I am, in the thick of another.'

Clive had no answer and wondered where this was leading and if he wanted to be involved.

The phone rang, startling both men from their thoughts.

'Hello,' said Paul, when he picked up the handset. 'Paul Thomas.'

'Mrs Cartingdon-Bligh . . .'

'Oh, it's you' interrupted Paul, 'trashing my house is not going to make any difference, just leave me alone or I'll call the police.'

'I don't know what you are talking about, Mr Thomas, are you telling me you have been burgled?'

'You know very well. I have told you, I know nothing of any, what did you say it was, a parcel or package, belonging to your, er, husband.'

'Let's not play games, Mr Thomas. Shall we say it will go no further if you leave the package at this address, have you got a pencil?' she paused, 'One

102

hundred-and-two, Hills Road, Cambridge. Ask for Andy, he knows to expect you. Oh, and if you don't hand it over, I know where you live. Goodbye, Mr Thomas.' Paul did not say a word while she was talking, and now he looked at Clive looking very worried.

'What is it?' asked Clive.

'It was her. She denies trashing the house, but she says she knows where I live. What next?'

'Do you think you had better hand it over?' asked Clive.

'What do you think?' said Paul, through gritted teeth.

'No, I guess not, so what *are* you going to do?'

14

Before either man had time to think what they might do, the phone rang again. Paul looked at Clive and picked up the handset.

'Yes, what now?'

'Mr Thomas?' a man's voice, pronouncing Thomas with the Th as in 'the'.

'Yes, who are you?'

'Who I am is not matter, Mr Thomas. You have somesing I want.'

'Oh, really, what is that?'

'I sink you know. Now, you can give it to me, or I will take it, and you would not like me to do that.'

'I have absolutely no idea what you are talking about, Mister, or should I say, Herr . . .'

'You have some minerals, Mr Thomas, and I want them. I am willing to pay fair price . . .'

Paul put down the phone, but before he could tell Clive what the call was, the phone rang again.

'Do not mess wiz me, Mr Thomas. I am serious. I will give you good price for ze box. You will meet me, yes?'

'I told you, I don't know what you are talking about,' said Paul and once more put down the phone. It rang again immediately.

'Mr Thomas, please. A good price, yes?'

'What do you call a good price?' said Paul, immediately realising his mistake.

'Ah, so now you do admit to having ze box! I will give you one hundred thousand euros for ze box, and no questions asked.'

'That's not enough.'

'Two hundred thousand.'

Paul was thinking he doubled his offer very quickly, he's obviously willing to go much higher. He was enjoying this.

'I want half a million,' said Paul.

'OK. So, shall we meet at the National Portrait Gallery in London, tomorrow at three in the afternoon. Goodbye, Mr Thomas.'

Paul put down the phone and turned to Clive.

'That was someone willing to pay half a million euros for the box, Clive. What do you say, two-fifty each?'

Clive was gobsmacked. 'You aren't going to sell it surely?'

'Why not, nobody knows I have it. At least only this foreign guy, and he won't tell anyone. What I would like to know is how does he know about the box? You don't think Tim would have told anyone?'

'Not Tim, no, I know him, Paul, he's a good guy.'

'But he might have just let slip something . . .This guy wants me to hand over the box tomorrow, in London, and he says he'll pay.'

'You aren't going to sell it, surely?' said Clive again.

'No, I'm not, but I want to see who this guy is, I'm going to the meeting place. Do you want to come?'

Clive had been thinking how he could make an excuse to get out of this situation. It was getting too much for him. He had wanted to help his friend but now it sounded dangerous and he was worried, but now Paul had put him on the spot.

'Just to see who he is, right?'

'That's all. I want to see who we are up against. And if it is someone from Jay-ems, you might just recognise him.'

'OK then, I'm with you. I'd better phone Jacqui to tell her I'll be a bit longer.'

'Will she mind?'

'She'll be all right – I hope.'

They decided to take the train down to London despite the cost, as they didn't fancy driving in the capital. It meant driving to Cromer as Hildisham's station closed in 1892. They would have to change at Norwich.

'Which station does the Norwich train go to?' asked Clive. 'Any idea?'

'Liverpool Street, I think. Then we can take the tube to Trafalgar Square. Have you got a tube map on your phone?'

Clive had, and after searching for a minute he suggested the best way was by Circle line to the Embankment. 'I don't think it's far from there to Trafalgar Square. We can walk.'

'Useful things, those fancy phones, I suppose I shall have to get one myself.'

Clive was still looking at his phone. He had called up a street map of London and could see that he was right. 'It isn't too far to walk, but I think a taxi would probably be the best bet.'

'Oh, good, so do you think we can get there by three?' Paul asked.

'Should just make it I think.'

'I hope so, I would hate to miss our mystery man after all that.'

They parked the car at the station and Clive used his phone to pay. Paul was amazed and once more declared his intention to buy a smart phone.

'I can't remember the last time I travelled by train,' said Paul, as they settled into their seats.

'It's a good way to travel but it is so expensive these days,' said Clive. 'We may as well enjoy it, I guess.'

The journey, including the change at Norwich was enjoyable and the two men were able to put to back of their minds the purpose of their train ride for a little while as they looked out of the window and watched the scenery go by.

It was easy to find a taxi at Liverpool Street, and in no time, they were deposited right outside the National Portrait Gallery.

'Have you ever been to this gallery?' Paul asked.

'Never have, been to the British and Science Museums and the Tate and such, but not here. Not really my thing.'

'Long time since I was here, but I don't suppose it has changed much, well worth a look. Come on, we've got time to find a spot where we can watch for our man.'

'How will you know him?'

'I'm hoping he will stand out like the proverbial thumb.'

'Not because he is foreign – the place will be full of foreigners,' suggested Clive.

'No, I think I will be able to spot him – you'll see.' Paul assured him.

They found a spot in the foyer, quite close to a display of postcards and a sign saying 'No photography'.

'It's coming up to three now, watch the door,' whispered Paul.

At ten minutes past three, Clive was wondering if they could have missed their man and was about to say something, when Paul gestured to keep quiet, 'Look', he said, pointing to a small man with a goatee beard, wearing a long black overcoat and carrying a small case. 'That's him, I'm sure of it.'

The man was standing by a bust in an alcove just off the main foyer area. He was looking all around him, but not moving from his spot.

'He does look a bit suspicious I must say. But not dangerous, do you think?'

'Hard to tell. I don't plan to find out. Now we know what he looks like, we are forewarned,' said Paul in a whisper. 'I am going to get a photo of him.' But when he took out his little digital camera, a man in a uniform appeared, 'No photographs, sir!'

While Paul was apologising, Clive had taken a quick snap with his phone and quickly put it away.

'Got him!' said Clive.

'What?'

'I've got a picture – with my phone,' said Clive, laughing.

'Oh, well done! That's us done then. That's what we came for.'

'Why don't we watch where he goes?' suggested Clive, as they were about to leave.

'What do you mean?' asked Paul.

'We know what he looks like, but it would help to see where he goes, don't you think?'

'Of course it would, good thinking!'

Making sure the man was still in his place they left, mingling with a crowd of Japanese tourists so they wouldn't be seen. They didn't know if the mystery man knew what they looked like.

There was no convenient place from which to observe the entrance to the gallery, so they walked up and down trying to look inconspicuous. They soon got tired however, and were about to give up when the little man came out of the building, looking right and left at the edge of the kerb. Almost immediately a black Mercedes saloon drew up and the man got in. The car sped away.

'Big help that was!' exclaimed Paul. 'We're no wiser.'

'We are! I got a photo!' said Clive, exultantly waving his phone. 'I got the man, the car reg and, with a bit of luck, the writing on the side of the car.'

'Let's see,' said Paul.

'Be better inside, too bright out here,'

'I know the very place, are you hungry?'

'Always - and thirsty.' Said Clive, smiling.

Paul led the way to the Admiralty, London's most central pub.

'Find a table, I'll be right with you,' said Paul as they entered the dark, wood panelled bar.

Before long they were eating the establishment's signature ale pie and chips and drinking pints of London Pride bitter.

'This is an unexpected treat,' said Clive.

'Yes, I always like to come here when I'm in London. You can watch all London going by from here.

When they had finished their meal and had started on their second pint of Fullers' prize-winning ale, Paul asked to see the photographs Clive had taken.

Clive handed the phone to Paul.

'Just hold it by the edges and do a kind of reverse pinch on the picture to make it bigger.'

It took Paul a few tries but when he had mastered the technique he was amazed at the clarity of the images of their quarry and of the car.

'I think you can just read what it says on the side of the car,' said Clive taking back the phone and squinting at the image.

'Trestenmetallurgisch-Ind.GmbH, I think it says.'

'Even better! Now we know what were up against. Will you be able to print them?'

'When we get back, of course,' Clive assured him. 'Worth coming?'

'Definitely! Mission accomplished,' Paul said, but added, 'or perhaps we should say, to misquote a famous statesman, it is not the end, but perhaps the beginning of the end.'

15

Paul was in buoyant mood when they arrived back in Hildisham, he had something to get his teeth into, a clue to follow up, he had his quarry in his sights. At last, he was closer to finding out about at least one of the people trying to get hold of the box.

When he put his key in the lock the door opened. He hadn't turned the key. The hair on the back of his neck prickled. Something was wrong. Turning to Clive, who was getting out of the car, he called, 'Stay back, Clive, there's something wrong here.'

'What is it?' asked Clive, ignoring the warning and joining Paul at the door.

'Another break in,' said Paul, cautiously pushing to door fully open and stepping inside.

To Clive the room looked perfectly normal, but to Paul it looked as if it had been picked up and shaken, moving everything very slightly from its place and put back down almost exactly – but not quite.

'They've been very careful, but the place has been thoroughly searched. It just doesn't feel right.'
quietly. He turned to Clive, who was looking worried. 'What is it, they've gone.'

'Listen, Paul, it's not that, I am not pulling out, believe me, but, it's like this – I am chairman of a group of steam enthusiasts called the Wednesday Afternoon Club, and we have arranged to show some of our engines at the Saffron Walden Steam Crank-up at the weekend, and, well . . .'

'You must go, of course, in fact I'll come, too!'

Clive had felt bad about leaving Paul at such a critical time and Paul had assured him that he was free to go at any time. 'Silly man!' he had said, slapping his friend on the back.

Paul drove Clive back home in time to make arrangements with his club members and agreed to meet him at the fair.

Paul drove to Saffron Walden early on Saturday. He enjoyed the ninety-mile drive on mostly quiet roads through the pleasant East Anglian countryside.

The Crank-up, at Carver Barracks on the site of the former Debden aerodrome, was not open to the public when he arrived but, when he explained he was with the Wednesday Afternoon Club he was admitted and told to park the car where there would be a display of classic cars, on one side of the main arena.

All morning steam engines of all shapes and sizes arrived and took up position alongside the arena. Stalls selling all manner of goods were set up and the food concessions began heating up their equipment. Every imaginable sort of food appeared to be on offer, from fish and chips to kebabs and everything else in between. By mid-day everything was ready and the field took on the look and feel of a cross between a fair and a circus. Paul was enjoying it immensely.

When Clive arrived, en-convoi with his club members and their engines, he was too busy to stop and talk to Paul, but waved to him when he spotted the TR.

More cars were arriving and to Paul's surprise and delight another TR7 drew up beside his and he and the driver began chatting. Then another favourite of Paul's, a Triumph Roadster arrived. Soon there was a sizeable contingent of desirable classics.

Crowds of people began flooding onto the field and the carnival atmosphere developed.

Many different steam powered vehicles joined the display and Paul was intrigued to see a First World War military steam engine pulling a heavy gun carriage. It had never occurred to him that steam vehicles would have been used in war.

There were stationary engines, too, showing off their ability to do all manner of tasks.

There were also displays and demonstrations and the whole day was full of noise and excitement.

The fairground organs provided a background sound and the many engines added their own distinctive noises. Paul wondered why he had never been to one of these steam gatherings before.

A large beer tent was attracting customers but Paul resisted. It would be too easy to get in among a crowd of enthusiastic beer drinkers.

Clive's Wednesday Afternoon club was involved in a demonstration, and as the engines drove round the arena, Clive, driving his big shiny Fowler engine, saw something disturbing. As he was about to come alongside the classic car display, he saw a man moving towards Paul's car, crouching low so as not to be seen. He was not concentrating of the direction his engine was going, he was so intent on watching the man, who appeared to have a gun in his hand. By now the engine was moving directly towards the man. He could see clearly as he got nearer that it was a gun and he had almost reached the TR where Paul stood watching the display.

Almost on automatic pilot, Clive opened the regulator, the chimney barked and there was whoosh of steam and a heavy ringing sound as the engine increased speed and headed for the man at full throttle. It was only at the last minute that the noise of the engine alerted the man and he turned in time to see the huge engine bearing down on him. He screamed, but it was too late, the offside front wheel of the engine struck him and he fell, the engine continued relentlessly and ran him over before stopping inches in front on Paul's TR, stopped only by a big pile of sandbags that marked the boundary of the classic car display. It all happened very quickly.

You wouldn't have to look very closely to see that the man was dead. It was not a pretty sight.

Everything went suddenly quiet as it was realised there had been a terrible accident. The only sound from the engine, now stopped, was a steady ticking as it cooled down.

The St John Ambulance team, who were on duty at the fair, were first on the scene but the accident was beyond their capabilities and they stood looking helpless while paramedics from nearby Saffron Walden dealt with the casualty.

Police, also on duty at the fair, appeared in force, and began questioning a number of witnesses.

Clive, looking very pale and worried despite having several young women trying to comfort him, was being questioned by a uniformed police sergeant.

Clive could not explain adequately what had happened. He had seen the man approaching his friend with a gun in his hand and he had acted instinctively, the engine seemed to take over, he said. But the policeman was not happy. He insisted on taking him to the police station. As the police would also want to question Paul, he, too was bundled into a police car and driven off.

'My name is Inspector Connors, and this is DS Roberts. What is your name?'

'Paul Thomas,' said Paul.

'Address?'

'Number one, Fishers' Lane, Hildisham, Norfolk.'

'Occupation?'

'Retired.'

'Retired what?'

'Just retired,' said Paul.

'What was your occupation, Mr Thomas?'

'I fail to see the relevance of that.'

'For the record, Mr Thomas.'

'Investigative journalist,' said Paul.

'I see, so you might have trodden on a few toes in that occupation, might you not?'

'Oh, yes,' said Paul, with a slight smile.

'So, do you think the man with the gun might have been someone you upset in the course of your – er – investigating?'

'It's possible, but I don't think so.'

'Why not?'

'Most of the bad guys I investigated are locked up!' This time Paul allowed himself a smile, 'Or dead.'

'This is serious, Mr Thomas.' The sergeant was getting impatient.

'Sorry,' said Paul. 'I have no reason to think the man was in any way connected with my activities as a journalist.'

'Thank you. So, shall we get on?' said the inspector.

'As you wish,' said Paul.

'Did you recognise the man?'

'I didn't look too closely at him, but I don't think I knew him.'

'And your friend, did he know the man?'

'I shouldn't think so.'

'What were you doing at the steam fair, Mr Thomas?'

'My friend was showing his engine, so I went along to watch.'

'Mr Flack lives in Cambridgeshire, Mr Thomas, quite a way from North Norfolk, how come you are friends?' interjected the sergeant.

'People move, Sergeant.'

'Very well. Now tell me again. Why the steam fair?' the inspector again.

'I like steam engines, my friend Clive runs a club for steam enthusiasts, he was showing his engine at the show, I went along. Simple as that.'

'So, you've no idea who the dead man is. And you've never seen him before.'

'That's right.'

'It's very strange, don't you think?'

'It is rather. What do you make of it, Sergeant?' said Paul, turning to face the other policeman.

'Is there any reason why anyone would want to harm you? Did you see the man coming towards you with a gun?'

The answer to all the questions was no. Paul had not seen the man until the engine had hit him. He had been watching the engines in the arena. And no, he said, he knew of no reason why anyone would want to harm him.

The inspector suddenly slammed onto the table a small black, slightly muddy, automatic pistol with a dark red Bakelite grip, which Paul instantly recognised as a Makarov, but when the inspector asked him if he had ever seen it before, he said, 'No, nasty looking thing. Is that the one that might have killed me?'

'Yes, it is, and I believe it is a Russian weapon. Why would a Russian want to kill you, do you think?'

'Absolutely no idea.'

Leaving Paul, the two detectives began questioning Clive, having sent the young women away.

'Of course I didn't want to kill him,' Clive was saying, 'I told you, I saw this man heading towards my friend with a gun, I just wanted to stop him.'

'Oh! You two are friends.' The sergeant exclaimed. 'I see, so why do you think your friend was in danger?'

'Well wouldn't you think someone was in danger if they were being approached by a man with a gun?'

'Yes, but why do you think anyone might want to harm your friend? It was not a random attack, was it?'

'No, but I don't know why he . . .' he stopped and looked the sergeant in the eye. 'I don't know, right!'

'Very well', said the inspector to the detective sergeant. 'We'll talk to them again later. Put this one in room two for now.'

'Let's see what they cook up between them,' he said to the DS, with an evil grin on his face.

16

Able at last to speak to each other, the two men sat on green rexine covered chairs in the bleak waiting room without, at first, saying much more than hello.

Paul was first to speak. 'It will be all right, Clive, they can't do you for anything.'

'I'm not so sure. I deliberately ran him down. They mentioned murder, Paul. What am I going to do?'

'I think we had better have a lawyer, do you know anyone?'

'I used to be very friendly with a QC who lived in the village, but he's dead now, so, no I don't. Do you?'

'I have had to consult lawyers from time to time, yes. Let me think who might be best.'

Paul was quiet for several minutes.

'Yes, I know the very man. Ian McFarland, he lives in Thetford. If I can remember his phone number . . .'

Clive looked on anxiously while Paul racked his brains.

'What are we going to say to these two coppers when they start questioning us again?' Clive asked.

'Nothing. Just say you've told them everything and you want to consult a lawyer,' Paul advised. Then, 'Got it! I knew there was a mnemonic to remember his number.'

'What was it?' Clive asked.

'Can't remember, but while I was trying to remember the mnemonic I remembered his number – Thetford 555754!'

Paul's lawyer friend, Ian McFarland, a solicitor with a practice in Thetford, was quick to respond. It isn't far from Thetford to Saffron Walden, and he was with the two unfortunate friends inside two hours.

While the two men related their version of events, he took notes.

'I think it's a case of accidental manslaughter. You shouldn't expect more than three to five years,' Mr Flack, and with good behaviour, you will be out in eighteen months.' He smiled benignly.

'What? You think I'll go to prison?' gasped Clive.

'Oh yes. You did kill a man,' said McFarland. 'You didn't expect to get off, surely?'

'Well, I was saving Paul's life, and, and the man I killed was a villain.' Clive was terrified at the thought of prison and was looking helplessly at Paul for him to say something.

'I will of course instruct a barrister to defend you. He will make sure you get a minimum sentence,' said McFarland.

'But I thought – I don't know, oh, God! What am I going to do? Look what you've got me into, Paul.'

Paul was equally horrified and didn't know what to say.

'I will be in touch. Good to see you, Paul. Goodbye to you both,' said the lawyer, and he left.

'Fat lot of good he was!' said Clive. He sat with his head in his hands.

Paul was thinking of other friends that he had got into terrible, sometimes life-threatening situations because of his actions, but this was worse, he could not do anything to console or comfort his friend.

Just then Inspector Connors came into the room, followed by DS Roberts bearing a tray of cups.

'I thought you two gentlemen might like a cup of coffee,' Connors said, smiling.

The detective sergeant put down the tray and handed cups of coffee to the two friends.

'Sugar and milk if you want it, and there are some biscuits. I'm sorry, the DC has eaten all the good ones,' said the inspector, smiling. The sergeant was also smiling.

'I'm sorry, gentlemen, forgive me,' the inspector went on, 'a witness has come forward and has given us a very good account of what happened. She was working on the hot-dog stand and had a good view. She saw the man creeping towards Mr Thomas, holding a gun. Before she could do anything to raise the alarm, the steam engine came, she used the word hurtling, but I think perhaps that was an exaggeration, towards the man with the gun, and well, you know what happened. The young woman is very happy to stand up in court and tell what she saw.'

'So, will I be charged?' asked Clive anxiously.

'That will be for the coroner to decide. I think it is unlikely. You will of course be required to attend the inquest, but for now, when you've finished your coffee and biscuits of course, you may go.' The inspector appeared to be pleased with the situation and the two men thanked him and the sergeant profusely.

Standing outside the police station a few minutes later Clive and Paul looked at each other.

Clive was very pale and Paul realised he was trembling. He put his hand on Clive's shoulder.

'Are you OK? You don't look so good.'

'I'm not,' said Clive, very quietly. 'I was terrified in there, I thought I was going to prison for murder.'

He raised his voice, almost hysterically, 'Don't you see! I can't do this any more, Paul. Take me home, I'm sorry.'

'I am sorry, Clive, it was all my fault. Of course, come on, let's find a bus to take us back to the car and I'll take you home.' He put his arm round his friend's shoulder and gave him a reassuring squeeze.

'I thought I was going to be locked up,' said Clive, quieter now. 'Do you think the police would give us a lift back to the car?'

'I think that might be pushing it. No, we'll get bus, there's bound to be one.'

They discovered that Stevenson's Bus Company ran a twice daily service to Carver Barracks where the steam fair was being held. They were just in time to catch it, and paid the driver the two-pound fare for the nine-minute journey.

Clive was quiet while they were on the bus, and Paul thought it best not to say anything. He felt bad about getting Clive into serious trouble and he was grateful for his action which might well have saved his life. But he had been in situations of extreme danger many times and was able to shrug off his brushes with the police. He realised his folly in getting his friend into danger and didn't know what to say.

Paul was relieved to see the TR still safely in its parking place and slid gratefully into the driver's seat. Clive got into the passenger seat, not wanting to drive. Neither man looked at the disturbed ground where the engine had run over the gunman.

'I hate it when I am parted from my car, it was my wife's you know,' Paul said, as he started the engine.

'You did mention it,' said Clive, smiling.

'You don't know how anxious I've been about it.'

'Not anxious about your friend who was going to prison for murder then?' quipped Clive.

'Of course. I was worried sick about that, you know that,' pleaded Paul.

Clive punched Paul's arm playfully but painfully.

'Are you OK?' asked Paul.

'I'm OK now, but I can't do it any more, really. I do want to go home.'

'Of course, I am so sorry, Home it is. What about your engine?

'Oh, that's OK, one of the guys from the club will see to it.'

It was clear to Paul just how worried Clive had been if he was willing to leave his engine in the hands of someone else. He felt about his engines the same way Paul felt about his TR7.

Clive was quiet for the first part of the journey back to Clive's home, but he suddenly started talking. Nervous reaction, Paul thought.

'I used to like travelling by bus in the old days, before I learned to drive, of course. Mind you, buses weren't as nice as this one,' Clive said, talking quickly, 'We went everywhere by bus, we knew all the times and the numbers. Favourite was Cambridge of course, we often went there, but Royston was nearest and our little local firm was best if you wanted to go there.'

'Buses are OK, but in those pre driving days I used to cycle everywhere,' said Paul, 'A friend designed a lightweight touring bike for me and I had it made up by a specialist bike shop. It cost me twice as much as my first car, but it was a beauty. I could cover long distances without getting tired. I wonder what happened to that bike?'

Clive didn't speak again, and Paul decided it was best to let him sit quietly. Neither of them spoke any more until they drew up outside Clive's house.

'Thanks Paul,' said Clive, getting out of the car. 'Are you coming in?'

'Best not, I think. You need to rest,' said Paul, not keen to face Clive's wife. 'See you!' he called as he drove off, waving as he went.

17

A few weeks later, Paul was summoned to attend the inquest on the would-be murderer who Clive had run down.

Paul had not seen or heard from Clive since he had dropped him off at home after the traumatic time at Saffron Walden and didn't know what to expect. He saw Clive across the foyer, standing talking to his wife. He waved, trying to catch Clive's eye.

Clive waved back and smiled, but didn't make any move to come over. Paul thought it best to leave it - for now anyway.

The inquest was a grisly affair, with photographs of the accident with close-ups of the crushed dead man shown to all concerned.

It had not been possible to identify the dead man but witnesses stated that he had been seen prior to the incident with the traction engine, carrying a gun in such a way as to indicate his intention to use it.

The young woman, who said her name was Maria Trevaunce, stated that she thought the man was aiming his gun at Mr Thomas, who she identified by pointing at Paul. She had not come forward immediately as she was busy with the hot-dog stand.

Clive had to give his account of the incident, and speaking quietly said he was sure his friend was in danger and that he had acted instinctively.

Paul was called and asked if he knew the deceased and if he was aware of any reason why the man wanted to harm him. Paul said of course he had no idea, and in fact had been unaware of the man coming towards him until the engine ran him down.

More witnesses were called, but none could offer any useful information. Nobody knew who the dead man was. Finger prints and dental records had failed to identify him. It was concluded that he was a foreign national. His next of kin could not be found and nobody had come forward to claim his body.

After deliberation, the coroner concluded that it was a case of death by misadventure and closed the court.

The police would continue their investigations but Clive was told he was not going to be charged and he was free to go.

Among the people mingling in the foyer after being dismissed by the court, Clive and Paul looked awkwardly at each other.

'Hello, Paul,' said Clive, 'How are you?'

'I'm OK, thank Goodness that's all over.'

'Yes, I've been so worried I would be held responsible. But death by misadventure lets me of the hook. I really thought I was done for.'

'I can't tell you how sorry I am for getting you into it, Clive. Can you forgive me?'

'Now I can, of course. But there was a time when your name was mud in my family, and I never wanted to see you again.' He laughed nervously.

'Perhaps I can come over some time and see more of your collection,' suggested Paul, cautiously.

'Yes, I'll look forward to it,' said Clive, but his wife was urging him to come away and he just gave a little wave and was lost among the little crowd of people.

Paul was feeling relieved, but unhappy to leave things unresolved as far his friendship with Clive was concerned. He left the court and returned home.

18

As soon as Paul drove onto the little gravel drive in front of his garage, he could sense something was amiss. He got out of the car and approached the front door of the cottage cautiously. He gave the door a little push, certain somehow that it would be unlocked. It is a strange phenomenon that criminals never seem to lock doors behind them.

In the living room sat a man Paul had never seen before.

'Who the hell are you?' exclaimed Paul. 'What are you doing in my house?'

'Calm down, Mr Thomas. Please. I am sorry for my unusual introduction. It was necessary for me to catch you at home.'

'Unusual you say! Breaking into my home! Who are you? What do you want?'

'I think you know what I want, Mr Thomas. My name is Andriej Rasanov. I represent a company called Trestenmetallurgisch of Hanover, Germany. We deal with rare earths and metals that are used in medical research and also in the communications industry. We are anxious to recover a box of rare metals that you have in your possession. I mean you no harm, Mr Thomas, but, if necessary, I can be quite persuasive.' The man had spoken in perfect unaccented English, so perfect in fact that he was clearly a foreigner, Paul thought. But who was the man on the phone and at the gallery? – he was from the same firm, perhaps he was just a messenger.

'What about the man who tried to kill me at the steam fair? Did he not mean me any harm?' said Paul.

'That was very unfortunate, I am sorry. The man exceeded his instructions. He won't bother you again.'

'That's a fact, he's dead!' said Paul, not without some satisfaction.

'Let's not be unpleasant about it, shall we? Just hand over the box and we need never see each other again.' The man had spoken quietly and evenly. But Paul had dealt with people like this before. They lull you into acceptance of their propositions, and before you know where you are you are at the bottom of a lake with heavy chains round your feet.

'How do I know you are the rightful owner of the samples?' Paul asked, after a long pause.

'You don't. But you had better believe it. Now, hand it over, Mr Thomas, last chance.'

'What are you going to do. Shoot me? That way you will never get the box. It is so well hidden you will never find it. I need proof that you are the rightful owner. Is that so difficult?'

'Think about it, Mr Thomas. Just think about it.'

Herr Rasanov, if that was his name, got slowly to his feet and walked towards the door, turning before opening it and repeated, 'Think about it, Mr Thomas.' He opened the door and went out, closing the door quietly behind him.

Paul was feeling very uneasy after the encounter, and wondered what threat was implied by the man's parting shot. He was thinking about it. He had to do something with the box. It was not his, nor had he any right to decide where it went, or to whom he gave it. But he felt sure the German was not the rightful owner, he could not explain, it was his instinct, an instinct that had led him to all manner of criminals in the course of his journalism.

'And what about the man who had offered half a million Euros for the box, was he an imposter? And Rasanov had not mentioned money. Which was the genuine employee of Tresten whatever it's called,' Paul muttered. 'Rasanov doesn't sound German to me.' He sat thinking for several minutes and then, suddenly, 'I'll go to Germany!' he exclaimed. Then realising he had spoken his thoughts aloud again, restrained himself. He thought the only way to find out for sure if Rasanov was genuine was to go Germany and investigate the company. 'Hanover,' he said to himself, 'I've never been there.'

He fired up his laptop and entered Hanover in Google maps. What's the best way to get there? Assuming the ferry would take him to The Hague, he entered 'The Hague to Hanover by train', and discovered that there was a regular train service with fares from twenty-five euros, 'what's that? Twenty quid. Cheaper than driving.' Not for the first time he was amazed how cheap rail travel was on the nationalised trains of Europe. He was still muttering; it was a habit he would have to try to stop.

He was still thinking about travelling to Hanover when the phone rang. Expecting it to be Rasanov again, he hesitated before answering.

'Yes!' he barked into the handset.

'Hello, is that Paul?' said a voice he recognised.

'Clive? Is that you? I'm sorry, I thought it might be someone I didn't want to talk to. Are you OK, good to hear from you.'

'I'm OK, thanks. I felt we parted in less than happy circumstances, I wondered how you are.'

'That's nice of you, Clive, considering what I put you through.'

'So, have you resolved the business with the box?'

'No, still got it and people want it. I don't know what to do. Actually, I have decided to go to Germany to find out a bit about the company that claims ownership. It's in Hanover.'

'Ooh, Hanover?'

'Yes, do you know it?'

'No, but they have a very big steam fair there; I've always wanted to go. It's this month actually, you should try to go while you are there. You'll see posters everywhere I expect, Zeche Hannover Dampfmaschinen Festival,' he recited the unfamiliar words carefully.

I doubt I'll have much time or opportunity to go to steam festivals, Clive, but thanks, I will look out for it.'

Clive was quiet for a few seconds. 'Are you driving?' he said at last.

'Driving? Oh, no. I thought I would go by train, it will be cheaper. It's only about twenty quid from The Hague.'

'What if I were to help with the petrol? Could I come too? Two people in a car would probably work out about the same cost.'

'No reason why you shouldn't come, I would like your company, but I fancied the train journey.'

'But you won't have transport when you get there.'

'You have a point. OK, I'll think about it.'

'The festival is next week actually. When are you planning to go?'

'As soon as possible, I guess. OK, you're on, Clive. Shall I come and pick you up?'

'No, I'll come to you. We can go in my car; probably more practical don't you think?'

'I don't know, what do you drive?'

'Kia Sportage, it's nice and roomy.'

Paul had no idea what a Kia Sportage was or what it was like, but if Clive was willing to drive all the way to Hanover in it, it must be OK, he guessed. So he agreed.

'I'll look into ferries in the meantime then, see you soon.'

With the aid of Google, Paul found the best way was in fact Harwich to the Hook and from there it was a more or less straight road to Hanover. He also found times of crossings and fares – a car and two passengers would cost about a hundred and sixty pounds for the outward voyage but strangely only hundred and twenty-five coming back. The voyage took almost seven hours. More searching revealed that Hanover was two hundred and seventy miles from The Hook with an estimated driving time of five hours. There was a sailing at nine in the morning so they would arrive in Hanover at about nine in the evening, just enough time to book into a hotel and get a meal. He wrote it all down and continued looking at the Hanover website. 'Might as well book a hotel while I'm on the internet,' he thought to himself, and eventually found a suitable hotel in the city centre called the Arthotel. He reckoned three nights would be long enough and booked, paying a reasonable three hundred Euros for both of them, hoping Clive would not mind sharing a room. He sighed and sat back, feeling pleased with his work.

Paul was not at all sure what he would do when he got to Hanover. The object of the trip was to investigate the metallurgical company, but how he would do that he had no idea. One thing he was sure of was that he would not involve Clive who would be safe at the steam fair.

The laptop was still open at the Google page and Paul thought it would help to find out where the firm was. He entered the name and it came up straight away in an industrial estate a few kilometres from the centre. 'There will be buses I expect, so that's good.' He was still speaking his thoughts out loud.

Clive arrived in his Kia Sportage very early on the following morning, looking eager. 'Are you fit? I've only packed enough for a few days, is that OK?'

'I'm hoping it won't take that long, I've booked a hotel for three nights. That should give you two days at the steam fair.'

'I tend to take rather longer usually. I take the caravan to steam fairs and I can stay as long as I like, but yes, two days is OK.'

Paul approved of the Sportage, it was, as Clive had said, roomy and comfortable. More so than Paul's tiny sports car.

They didn't say much before reaching Harwich. It was a bit early in the morning for Paul. He was used to getting up around half past eight since retiring.

Getting aboard was a simple matter and they both agreed it was easier than flying. They found some comfortable reclining seats and settled down for the crossing.

At about midday, Clive nudged Paul, who had fallen asleep, and suggested breakfast, or lunch, whatever you might call it at that time of day.

The restaurant was good and they enjoyed a full English breakfast, a treat for Paul who usually had only a bowl of cereal or toast for breakfast, if any.

After eating, they went up on deck. They were still only half way through the voyage, in the middle of the North Sea; there were lots of ships going in different directions to their own. Paul was fascinated – he loved watching ships and could have stayed there, but Clive was finding it a bit too blowy and suggested they find a bar.

The rest of the day, with frequent visits to the bar or the restaurant, went quickly enough, and when they docked in the late afternoon, Clive was still feeling fresh enough to contemplate the five-hour drive to Hanover.

'We could stop somewhere for refreshments, it will still not be too late to check in to the hotel,' suggested Paul.

'We'll see how it goes. I don't mind driving all the way. It's fairly straightforward, and I've put it in the satnav. We go through some familiar sounding places, we might think about stopping at some of them on the way back, what do you think?'

'Sure, I'm easy,' said Paul. 'I bought some chocolate and some crisps to nibble.'

Passing through Rotterdam, Utrecht, Arnhem, Osnabruck and Minden, Paul thought of the wartime events which had made those names familiar to students of recent history.

It was easy to find the hotel, in the city centre. The two men were interested to see so many modern buildings and hardly any old ones, apart from some preserved ruins. The city had been targeted in the war and almost all of its old buildings had been destroyed.

'It makes you think, doesn't it?' said Clive, 'We thought we had it bad in the war, but we gave back a lot more. German cities were virtually wiped from the map.'

'It's a wonder they even speak to us, let alone wanting to be friends,' mused Paul.

'But they do, I've never been made more welcome anywhere,' said Clive.

The hotel was modern and clean and the room was fine. Clive said he didn't mind sharing as it was a twin-bedded room. He would have baulked at sharing a double!

After breakfast of cold meat and lightly boiled eggs, which neither man liked very much, they planned their day. Clive would need the car to get to the steam fair, and Paul was happy to make use of the city's excellent bus service.

'See you back here this evening then, what time shall we say? Seven?' said Clive. 'Then find a nice restaurant.'

'Sounds good. Have a good day, said Paul.

'Happy hunting, or should I say sleuthing?'

'Yes, I guess that's right. Bye then.'

When Paul arrived at the industrial estate, he began to feel apprehensive. He hadn't thought through how he was going to investigate the company.

He found it easily enough. It was a large glass clad building, very much like so many buildings he had seen in the city centre. A large notice board proclaimed the name and a list of senior staff names and their departments.

'That's helpful,' thought Paul. 'Is Herr Rasanov there?'

Scanning through the unfamiliar names, Rasanov didn't immediately stand out, but it was there, near the bottom. 'Andrej Rasanov, Kernspaltung.'

'Kernspaltung, what's that? Paul wondered. Other names had words after them, such as; Funkaktiv, Seltene Metalle, Rattination, Goldbarren, Elektronik, Auslandsverteilung, Medizinische Anwendungen. Most of which meant little to Paul, although he had a fairly good command of everyday German, technical terms were unfamiliar.

Paul decided his best bet was to find out about Herr Rasanov first. Would he be here, or was he still in England.

Still wondering what Kernspaltung meant, he once again wished he had invested in a smart phone which would have told him the meaning instantly. He did however have his little basic phone with Clive's number stored. He phoned Clive.

'Trouble already?' quipped Clive.

'No, would you ask your phone what Kernspaltung means?'

'No need, old friend, it means nuclear fission.'

'How do you know that?' exclaimed Paul.

'I know lots of things! That's what it means, I'm sure. I must have come across it somewhere.'

'How's the fair?'

'Great! There's lots to see. You must come, Paul.'

'Good, see you later then, and thanks for the translation.'

19

Faced with the prospect of actually finding Herr Rasanov in his office, Paul was mentally rehearsing what he might say.

Walking confidently up to the reception desk and feeling sure the receptionist would speak English, he didn't even attempt to speak German beyond a polite greeting.

'Guten morgen. I would like to see Herr Rasanov please.'

'Good morning, sir, one moment.' The young woman consulted a screen.

'I'm very sorry, Herr Rasanov is away on business. Had you arranged to see him?'

'No, but I have some important information for him.'

'If you would like to leave it with me, I will be sure to give it to him when he returns,' said the woman pleasantly.

'No, it is very sensitive, I would need to see him. Could I possibly speak to his secretary?'

'I should think that would be possible. Bear with me a moment.' She consulted her screen again and then picked up a telephone. Speaking in rapid German that Paul could not grasp, the woman turned to him and smiled. 'You can see Fraulein Gossen now. It's room 24, on the first floor. The stairs are there,' she pointed, 'or you can use the lift which is a little way along the corridor there,' she pointed again. 'I will give you a visitor badge. What is your name?'

Reluctant to give his real name, Paul hastily invented an alias for himself. 'Robert Hillman,' he said.

Armed with his visitor badge, Paul headed for the stairs, but seeing several people descending, changed his mind and went towards the lift.

Luckily, the lift was unoccupied. Paul didn't want to risk being seen by too many people in case they were able to remember him.

Herr Rasanov's office was one of only four on this floor. It suggested to Paul that it must be large and therefore occupied by an important employee.

He knocked and walked in. He was greeted by Fraulein Gossen, a smartly dressed middle-aged woman with grey hair scraped back severely and wearing no discernible makeup. This added to Paul's impression that Rasanov was an important part of the company and not too concerned with appearances.

'Herr Hillman. How can I help you?' she said in perfect but slightly clipped English.

'I was hoping to see Herr Rasanov and came on the off chance I would find him here,' began Paul, 'I have some information that I think he will find interesting.'

'You can leave it with me, it will be quite safe, and I will give it to Herr Rasanov when he returns.'

'How can I be sure it is safe? It is very, er, sensitive information.'

'I will put it in the safe, here, I will show you,' she walked to a bookcase, pulled it and it opened like a door, revealing a safe set into the wall. 'There, you see. Very secure,' she smiled for the first time. It transformed her face and Paul could see that she was actually very attractive, or could be if she took a little trouble.

'Thank you. Then if you would be so good as to put this in the safe for me.' Paul handed her a thick envelope that he had prepared for this eventuality. It contained nothing but several sheets of copy paper folded in to three.

The secretary took the envelope and with her back to Paul, opened the safe and put the envelope inside. 'There,' she said, closing the safe and

146

twiddling the combination dial. 'Safe, in the safe!' she smiled again.

'You are very kind, Fraulein.' said Paul.

'It's Frau, actually,' she said. 'It's company policy to employ single women. It's a security thing. But I have known Herr Rasanov a long time and he bended the rules,' she laughed. It had been the first time her English had not been absolutely perfect. Paul smiled and thanked her again.

Now that he had established that Rasanov was in fact an employee of the metallurgic company, and an important one at that, a plan was festering in Paul's mind and it was coming together nicely.

He had to wait a long time for a bus back to his hotel as the service was intended mainly for employees of the industrial estate. It gave him time to think his next move.

At last, back in his hotel room, he phoned Clive.

'Hi, Clive, how's it going?'

'Oh, it's a super fair, Paul, they've got everything here, there are even English classic cars, I've been talking to a young lady with beautiful red hair who owns an Austin Healey hundred, she's driven all the way from the south of Italy to be here. You'd love it, Paul. How are you getting on?'

'I'm not surprised you've found yourself a redhead, you old rogue,' said Paul, laughing. 'I'm OK, I've made some progress; I just need some time to think through my next move.'

'Why don't you come to the fair, relax and enjoy yourself for once.'

'I think I will, Clive, shall I meet you there?'

'Yes, of course. When do you think you can get here? There's a bus service specially for the fair from the bus station. I'll wait at the entrance. You can phone me when you are on your way.'

'Excellent!' said Paul. I'll just have a bite to eat and I should be there within an hour or so. Cheers.'

Grateful for an opportunity to forget the accursed box for a while, he looked forward to seeing the relics that Clive was so fond of.

20

It was early afternoon when Paul arrived at the show-ground. Clive was waiting as promised and Paul was not surprised to see an attractive youngish woman on his arm. How does he do it? Paul wondered as he waited to be introduced.

'Look who I met!' Clive exclaimed, 'This is Muriel, she lives in Wendy, would you believe?'

Paul shook Muriel's hand. 'Good to meet you, Muriel, what brings you to Hanover?'

'Sorry about the dirty hands, Clive dragged me off my engine to meet you.' She made a show of wiping her oily hands down her jeans.

'Your face is dirty, too,' laughed Clive.

'Oh, you rotter,' Muriel said, punching Clive, 'you didn't tell me before I met your friend.'

'He won't mind, will you, Paul?' said Clive, still laughing.

'So, what's the plan?' Paul asked.

Clive was keen to show his friend some of the treasures on show, so the three of them set off to do a tour of the exhibits.

'What happened to your Italian friend?' Paul whispered.

'Oh, she's still here, you may meet her later,' Clive grinned with a twinkle in his eye. 'Not a word to Jacqui!'

Paul was surprised at the size of the show-ground that appeared to be full of all manner of steam powered vehicles, all sending forth smoke and steam in equal measures. The noise was amazing, the engines had a life of their own and each one had a unique voice. Grimy, overall-clad men and women tended their machines and were keen to tell anyone who was remotely interested everything about them.

There was, as Clive had said, a display of vintage and veteran cars, and sure enough there were numerous English examples.

Catering stalls provided a mind-boggling selection of fast food from all corners of the world. The smells were intoxicating.

Clive persuaded Paul to try the sausages. Bratwurst they called them, long and fat, glistening and enticing, these traditional German delicacies were as delicious at they looked. Paul tucked in enthusiastically, even though he had already eaten.

There was an option to have sauerkraut with the sausage, but Paul had eaten that particularly German delicacy before and was not keen to repeat the experience.

Fairground organs, a German invention, playing traditional music, were there in strength, adding to the carnival atmosphere.

For a while Paul was able to forget the reason he was in Hanover. He was enjoying himself more than he had for a long time. He was also enjoying the company of Muriel.

By the time it had begun to get dark the three friends were beginning to flag. They made their way reluctantly to the car park. Muriel had a caravan on site, so bade the two men goodbye with the promise to see them again soon.

The fair had the atmosphere of a mediaeval army preparing for battle, with its tents and flags and the glow from so many boiler fires. It really was magical.

Clive was keen to hear Paul's news and what he was planning to do now he was in Hanover.

Paul didn't have a great deal to tell; he hadn't thought through what he would do, faced with the prospect of facing Herr Rasanov on his home ground. It was typical of him not to think through his methods of acquiring information. When he was working as an investigative journalist, he would follow up a situation that looked wrong to him and it had very often led him into very difficult and even life-threatening situations. He had also had many brushes with the police as a result of his work. Now, having decided to retire, he was perhaps a little more cautious and as a result, had not done anything too risky so far.

Paul told Clive of his visit to the headquarters of Trestenmetallurgisch Industries, and that he had deposited a bogus document so that he could see where documents were kept that might help to determine the validity of the company.

'What, do you plan to break in to the safe?' said Clive, horrified.

'I need to know if the firm is on the level before I can hand over the box. It is so valuable, and the specimens are potentially sensitive – possibly with military connotations. I just can't take the risk of them falling into the wrong hands.'

'Gosh!' said Clive, momentarily lost for words.

'Yes, Gosh. It is potentially very serious, I believe. I am going to have to be extremely careful.'

'Shouldn't you tell the police?' said Clive, looking very concerned.

'I don't have much faith in the police, I'm afraid, and I doubt they would believe me. All I have is suspicions. I need some more evidence, then I might consider going to the police. What I might do is leave a sealed envelope with them with details of my suspicions and also my plans to investigate the possible significance of the samples. If I don't come back, you could instruct them to open it.'

'If you don't come back! For goodness' sake Paul, don't do anything dangerous.'

'I hope it won't be dangerous, but just in case, will you inform the cops?'

'Me? Oh, well yes of course I will. Can you tell me what your plans are?'

'Not really, I don't want to put you in danger and the less you know the better.'

'You don't really think you could be in danger, do you?' asked Clive, increasingly concerned.

'If I were caught breaking in, of course I would, and if they are not kosher, they will not want to involve the police. They may take drastic measures to protect whatever it is they are doing.'

'What makes you think they are not, kosher, as you put it?

'Everything, I was chased by a motorcyclist in Spain, he was clearly intent on causing me harm. The way they kept phoning me with veiled threats, the fact that the package was given to me to smuggle out of Spain with instructions to take great care of it. The offer of a large sum of money for the box, an offer I doubt very much would have materialised. And my house being broken into – all those things, and my own instinct, which is rarely wrong.'

'It's frightening, Paul. If you are right, I don't think you should be putting yourself in danger.'

'I feel I must, Clive. It's what I do, or at least what I always did. I have decided to retire, but I can't leave this.'

'What can I do to help?'

'I can't allow you to get involved, Clive. You have family to think of. It will be good to know you are here while I try to find some information. But whatever might happen to me, please say nothing to anyone. That could put you in danger, and I couldn't bear that. I have put friends in danger before and I have no intention of ever doing it again.'

'I have to say, Paul, that I am very unhappy about all this. Please take great care, don't take unnecessary risks.'

Paul was touched by his friend's concern and patting him affectionately on the shoulder assured him that he would be careful.

In reality, Paul knew that he was putting himself in danger. Even if it turned out that the firm was legitimate, if he was caught breaking in, he would face prison. If, on the other hand, there were grounds for concern, the result of being caught would almost certainly be very severe indeed. He tried not to think about it.

21

Nothing more was said about Paul's mission. The two friends decided to make the most of their visit to Hanover and have a good meal in the city centre.

The hotel receptionist recommended the Gondola Restaurant in the city centre. Close to the GOP theatre and the Opera, the restaurant is popular with showbiz personalities. The two men thought it sounded expensive but they thought why not.

The restaurant, though quite old, had a very modern interior, its main dining area had widely spaced tables and there was an air of luxury.

Quickly shown to a table they were asked first if they would like to order aperitifs. Neither Paul nor Clive fancied aperitifs and ordered beer.

When presented with the menu they were baffled by the unfamiliar dishes on offer. Clive chose schnitzel because he recognised it, and when he asked the waiter what it was, Paul settled on Sauerbraten with potato dumpling, boiled potatoes and red cabbage.

As both meals went well with beer, they refused wine. For pudding they both had pumpkin tart.

The bill was even more than they had anticipated but they agreed it was worth it. They had enjoyed the food immensely and the service had been impeccable.

Relaxing with coffee in the hotel lounge later, it would have been easy to forget why they were in Hanover, but Paul sat up suddenly and declared, 'Right, action stations.'

'What?' said Clive.

'I must get on. I have to find out about this company and whether or not I hand over the box.'

'Oh, right, of course. What can I do to help?'

'You can't, I can't put you at risk. I've told you. And what I'm thinking of is going to be very risky indeed.'

Clive looked worried. He wanted to help Paul but was not keen to get involved with anything really dangerous, he did, as Paul had said earlier, have family to consider. Some of the tales Paul had been telling him of his exploits when he was an investigative journalist had horrified him, but even so he felt he should help if he could.

'Are you sure there's nothing I can do, Paul?' he asked.

'I'll let you know when I know myself what I'm going to do. I have to get a look inside that safe. I'm sure there will be clues in there. But how do I get into it?'

'Have you done a lot of safe-breaking?' asked Clive, with a small laugh.

'Not a lot, but I've had to open one or two.' Paul was not laughing. 'I'm going to my room to think, Clive, if you don't mind. I need to be quiet.'

'That's OK, I'll go for a bit of a walk before turning in. See you in the morning.'

Next morning, when the two friends met for breakfast, Paul outlined his plan for getting into the safe in Herr Rasanov's office. Clive thought it not only very risky, but not very likely to succeed.

Paul spent most of the morning using the hotel's computer and photo-copier, putting together a convincing set of documents that might just get him out of trouble should the need arise. These, along with a well-used false passport in the name of Doctor Philip Newman, he put in his briefcase. He was ready.

Paul ate very little lunch and didn't taste what he did eat. He was more worried about this venture than he cared to admit. He tried to put on a brave face for the sake of his friend.

Clive was still saying he wanted to help.

'You can drive me to the industrial estate, Clive, but then you must leave. I'm going to hide until it's safe to try to get into the office. Take the car back to the hotel and come back after about seven o'clock, by which time most if not all employees should have left the building.

'OK, but for goodness' sake take care!'

When they arrived at the industrial estate at about three in the afternoon, Paul left Clive, reminding him to come back later.

Adopting a different approach this time, Paul strode confidently up to the reception desk, smiling at the receptionist.

'Guten Tag. Ich würde gerne Herrn Rasanov sehen.'

'Guten Morgen, Sir, haben Sie einen Termin?'

'Nein, aber Ich habe wichtige Informationen für ihn.'

'Sehr gut. Wie heißen Sie?'

'Mein Name ist Doktor Philip Newman.'

'Ich werde mich erkundigen, ob er dich sehen wird.' The young woman consulted a screen.

'Herr Rasanov ist nicht hier, aber Sie können seine Sekretärin sehen.'

'Vielen Dank. Wo ist ihr Büro?'

'Im ersten Stock, Zimmer Nummer Vierund-zwanzig. Warten Sie, ich werde Ihnen einen Besucherausweis geben.'

Handing Paul a plastic badge with his name on it, the receptionist smiled. 'Guten Tag, Herr Doktor.'

Feeling pleased with his performance and relieved that it had been a different young woman on reception, Paul made his way to the lift, realising too late that he hadn't asked where it was.

Arriving on the first floor, the second part of his plan would be tested.

He had noticed, when he was here before, a fifth door, in addition to the four numbered offices, that had no number. He hoped it was a caretaker's storeroom and not a toilet. He tried the handle, the door opened. It was dark inside, good so far, he closed the door and felt for a switch and switched on the light. It revealed a small room, not much bigger than a cupboard, with shelves full of office materials. Packets of copy paper, printers and printing ink cartridges for several brands of printer, toilet rolls, stacks of coloured cardboard, a whiteboard and easel with packets of markers. Also, many boxes with their contents written in German that Paul could not interpret. Everything in fact that you would need in an office.

Paul could not have been more pleased. His plan was going well so far. He could hide in this room until the offices closed. He just had to hope that nobody would need any of the materials in the storeroom. Finding some substantial boxes to sit on, and switching off the light, he settled in for a long wait.

It was not long before he wished he had waited until later in the afternoon to hide in the cupboard. He could not risk putting on the light in case it was noticed from outside, and sitting uncomfortably in the dark, time seemed to drag. He could just make out the time on his luminous watch dial. After an hour he stood and stretched his legs, and in so doing he dislodged some boxes from a shelf, making a noise he thought must have been heard outside. He held his breath, fearful of discovery. What could he say in his defence? Nothing. He was doomed, and despite his situation he smiled at the phrase, made famous by the character in the television programme, Dad's Army. That thought actually cheered him. Nobody had come rushing to see what was happening in the storeroom, nobody had heard. The chances of someone being in the lobby to the offices at that precise time were small. He was OK. He thought about his next move. He had with him tools for opening locks, tools that had served him well for years; he felt confident they would get him into Rasanov's office. He was a little less confident about being able to open the safe. He had opened safes before; most safes were in fact not very safe if you knew enough about them. But would this one be a more sophisticated modern one that he could not open. It remained to be seen. If he could not open it, there may be documents in the office that would help. He looked at his watch again. Another hour had passed. Not long now, he thought.

At half past six, when he reckoned most office workers would have left the building, he opened the door of his hiding place and peeped out. All was in darkness.

He listened. There was no sound. He ventured out and with his little torch sought room four.

The lock looked conventional, he selected a slim stainless probe and inserted it into the keyhole, twisting it to feel the tumblers. When he was sure what needed to be done, he inserted another probe and after a few seconds the lock clicked. He pushed down the door handle and it opened. No alarm sounded. This was something he had worried about, as there was nothing he could have done to stop it had there been one.

He entered the office and pulled open the bookcase that hid the safe. It was mounted on wheels, hidden when closed, so it swung open easily. The safe was quite small. An office like this would not need a large safe. It had a keyhole and a numbered dial. First, he applied his probes to the keyhole. Often safes have a strangely shaped key, designed to make it difficult to open, but Paul had come across them before, the actual locks are often not very complicated. The lock clicked. He then concentrated on the combination. With his ear close to the door, he turned the dial, listening for the tumblers. He had no way of knowing how many numbers there were in the combination but worked on the premise that there would be four. When the fourth tumbler clicked, he took a deep breath and pulled the lever. The door swung open. 'Phew!' he said. Then realising he had spoken aloud again, looked round anxiously.

Most of the papers in the safe were in German and although his German was quite good, he found it hard to understand the technical terms.

There was a small bundle of Euros and some other currencies and a cash tin which rattled when he shook it. Petty cash, he thought. Just as he was thinking this had been a waste of effort and he was no wiser, he spotted a small stack of letters, held together with staples. Shining his torch and looking closer he could see the letter heading in Cyrillic script: Военный Исследование Институт. 'Aha!' said Paul, aloud again, 'this is interesting.' He took out his little digital camera and photographed several of the letters and what he took to be copies of the replies from Herr Rasanov, also in Cyrillic, but on the German firm's headed notepaper.

162

Not having any idea of the significance of his find, but feeling he may be getting somewhere, he put everything back as near as possible to how he found it and closed the safe, giving the dial a little spin. He could not relock it. He returned the bookcase to its normal position.

He then had to think how he was going to get out. Sometimes getting out was just as difficult as getting in. Doors would be locked and there may be a security guard. He had not thought this through, so keen had he been on getting in to Rasanov's safe.

He went to the window and looked out. It was too high on the first floor to consider jumping out, even if he could open the window, but he tried to open it anyway. The windows were designed to open just enough to let in some air, but on closer examination he could see that the entire pane could be lifted out, for cleaning no doubt. Once out, the opening was big enough to get through. He leaned out and could see the roof of an extension only a few feet below him. Carefully placing the pane against the wall, he climbed out and lowered himself onto the sloping roof. From there it was a simple matter to drop to the ground.

Not sure now where he was in relation to the entrance, Paul crept along the side of the building, keeping clear of windows, just in case there was a security guard who might just happen to look out.

Having traversed two sides of the building he could see the entrance gates, which were of course closed. A high chain link fence surrounded the building and the gates were evidently the only way in.

It was not unusual for Paul to miss a vital part from his plan, if he'd even had a plan. This time he had missed out a big part. Too late, he thought he should have gone back to his hiding place and simply walked out when the offices opened again in the morning. But that would not have worked, suppose the caretaker had needed something from the store.

Everything had gone smoothly so far and now he was going to be defeated by a simple fence. There was no way he could climb over, or open the electrically operated sliding gates.

Barely an hour had passed since he had entered the office. How long would he have to wait before a car came through? Probably not until the morning. And even then, the chances of being able to slip through before the gates closed again and without being seen were slim.

It seemed there was nothing he could do but wait and hope for the best. He crawled under a large decorative bush, one of several at intervals around the building and fifty or so yards from the entrance, and tried to make himself comfortable.

It was times like this that he wished he still smoked. It was thinking of smoke that gave him the idea. Gathering some leaves that had collected under the bush and stayed dry, he lit them; he always carried his lighter because it had been a gift from Laura, and he liked the feel of it, it was like a worry bead that he had rubbed until it was perfectly smooth.

The leaves were reluctant to burn but they did produce a lot of smoke, just what Paul had hoped. He broke off some small twigs from the bush and soon had a little fire going, producing copious amounts of smoke. But on its own this was not enough. He needed to create enough smoke to make someone call the fire service. Feeding more wood to the blaze, things were looking promising. He needed to get the fire big enough for the guard, for there must be one, to call the fire engine. The bush itself was now burning furiously and flames were licking the cladding of the building. Paul had nowhere to hide.

He suddenly remembered that Clive would probably have returned by now. If only he could attract his attention.

With his torch, Paul began a series of flashes pointing at the car park, where there were only one two cars, one of which he hoped desperately was Clive's Kia.

Clive had been watching for Paul ever since returning, and had seen the fire. He didn't at first see the flashes as it looked as if they were caused by the fire. He didn't think it could be Paul, but when the flashing continued, he decided to investigate.

He walked cautiously towards the entrance.

'Clive! Over here!' Paul called. 'Near the fire!'

Clive could not see Paul through the smoke but went closer.

'Here!' said Paul again. 'I can't get out.'

'What's with the fire?' asked Clive.

'I started it. I wanted to get someone to call the fire engine. I have to get them to open the gates.'

'What can I do?'

'Gather as much rubbish as you can and help me to make the fire bigger.'

Clive went off and after a few minutes returned, carrying a rubbish bin that he had found by the entrance to the car park. 'It's pretty full of all kinds of rubbish but it's too heavy for me to throw over.'

'That's OK, just feed the stuff though the fence to me.'

It was a very unpleasant job for Clive because there was all manner of rubbish, including banana skins, cigarette butts, and even a soiled nappy, but dutifully, Clive posted it all through the fence and Paul added it to the fire which by now was giving off clouds of noxious smoke.

He mingled with a small crowd that had materialised from somewhere and he was able to join Clive. They tried to look part of the crowd.

It was not long before an alarm sounded and floodlights went on all around the building, half a dozen or so men from the company began milling round and Paul contrived to be part of the mêlée.

Soon the wail of the fire engine could be heard. In the confusion it was possible for Paul to slip through the gates when they opened for the fire engine to come through.

Police cars soon appeared, and uniformed officers added to the growing crowd of onlookers.

'The fire engine got here quickly,' said Clive.

'My guess is that the company is on their priority list,' said Paul, 'let's get away quickly.'

22

Much to Paul's surprise, it was still only eight o'clock when they got back to the hotel.

'I need to get cleaned up,' said Paul.

'Me, too, I stink worse than I do after a day's steaming,' laughed Clive. 'See you in a bit.'

When they had cleaned themselves up and recovered a little from the excitement, the two friends sat in the hotel bar drinking beer, which they compared to its English equivalent.

'Well, of course there is no comparison is there,' began Clive, 'I mean, imagine a pint of Doom Bar, fresh from the cellar, temperature forty-two degrees, nice head on it, and then this stuff, it's got a head, that's obvious, it's too much, but it's too cold for a start and there's not a lot of taste in it. I don't know about alcohol content, but judging by the size of the glasses and the amount they put away, it's not a lot better than lemonade, with perhaps a tiny dash of something to give it a bit of colour.'

'I think you are being a bit harsh,' said Paul, 'it has a clean fresh taste, and it's quite refreshing. After a litre or two, I find you don't much mind anymore that it isn't Doom Bar or Wadworth's Six x.'

'Wadworth's Six x.' what's that?'

'You don't see it often, it was one of my wife's favourites,' said Paul, with that dreamy expression he had on his face when he talked about Laura. 'You tend to see it in the west country.'

'English beer is definitely best,' asserted Clive, taking another swig from his enormous glass.

'Of course it is, but what I'm saying is, this isn't bad when you get used to it.' Paul put down his now empty glass and asked Clive if he would like another.

'Oh, go on then,' said Clive, laughing.

Armed with fresh foaming glasses the two settled down for a session, but then Clive remembered. 'Are you going to tell me what happened?'

'Oh yes!' replied Paul, still looking rather bleary eyed from the effects of the smoke.

Paul related his foray into the depths of the Trestenmetallurgisch building. He showed Clive the photographs of the documents in the safe on his camera. 'Look at this letter in particular – it's all in Russian,' he paused for effect.

'What does it say?' Clive asked.

'I've no idea, I don't know any Russian and I can't read Cyrillic script, so I don't know what the name of the company is either. But Russian – why is Rasanov dealing with Russia, it looks dodgy to me.'

'It might not be Russian, other countries use the Cyrillic alphabet,' said Clive.

'So they do, I hadn't thought of that. I bet it is Russian though. We need to find someone who can read it.'

'Rasanov sounds Russian to me, didn't you think so?'

'I suppose it does, I hadn't really thought about it, thinking of him as being German, but you're right. That would explain a lot,' Paul agreed.

'I know some people in Cambridge, they would probably know someone in the university who would be able to read Russian,' offered Clive.

'Yes, but we're in Germany,' countered Paul.

'We'll be going back soon,'

'Sorry, of course, I'm impatient, but yes it will have to wait until we get back. Having said that, there's nothing to keep us here now – have you seen enough steam engines?'

'Never enough if you have steam in your blood, but I guess so.'

'Better pay the bill then, and go.'

With some reservations they agreed that their brief stay in Germany had, for different reasons, been a successful venture.

It had also cemented the friendship between the two men. Paul had enjoyed Clive's repartee, and Clive had been interested to hear of Paul's adventures.

'Do they serve English beer on the ship?' asked Clive, as they got into the Kia.

'Shouldn't think so, Stena is Swedish surely. Don't you remember, we had Swedish beer coming over.'

'Never mind, soon be back home and a decent pint.' Clive sighed.

23

Many tiring hours later, Clive drew up outside his house. 'Are you coming in?' he asked.

'No, best be off. Thank you so much, Clive, old chum. You've been a great help. I need to get on with this this but as soon as it's over, we'll get together properly and you can show me all those wonderful engines.'

'It has been good, Paul, I have enjoyed your company. I have to say, I'm glad it's over though. I was very worried about you. Please take great care, and let me know how you get on.'

'Will do. Love to Jacqui. Bye!'

Paul had not been expecting a warm welcome from Jacqui, so made a cowardly departure.

By the time Paul parked the TR in front of his cottage he was pretty well all in. He had been foolish to continue the journey without a break at Clive's house, but he had been keen to get home and make plans for the next step of his investigation.

The house looked untouched. There had been no more break-ins. There was a pile of post on the mat. He picked it up and put it on the table where the bottle of Jamieson's still stood after Clive had made coffee. It was too tempting. Paul found a glass and poured himself a generous measure. His resolve to give up alcohol had been forgotten while they were away, so, he thought, what's the harm.

He took the drink and the post into his little office.

The post was the usual mix of bills and advertising matter, and two from charities asking for money.

He threw the opened envelopes and their contents into the bin. Might as well ask the postman to put it all straight into the recycling bin, he thought.

He took a sheet of copy paper from a pile rescued from his wrecked printer and with pen poised, began to think of his next move. But before he had written a word, the doorbell rang.

'Yes?' he said, to the man standing a pace from the door when he opened it.

The man was tall, about thirty, Paul guessed, and dressed in a fawn trench-coat. Austin Reed, thought Paul, smiling.

'Mr Thomas? May we come in?'

Paul had not seen the other man, who had been crouching, looking at the TR.

'What do you want?' asked Paul.

'Just a word, if we may,' said the man, pushing past Paul. The other man followed.

'Who are you, what do you want? You can't just barge in.'

'We can, Mr Thomas, we can,' said the first man. 'MI6,' he briefly flashed an ID card. The other man flashed his.

'MI6, for goodness' sake, what business have you coming here?' Paul was annoyed and beginning to feel threatened.

'We've been watching you, Mr Thomas.'

'Oh, why?'

'You know very well, why, Mr Thomas.'

Paul wished he wouldn't keep saying Mr Thomas like that. It felt like an attack. 'I have no idea,' he said.

'As I said, Mr Thomas, we have been watching you.'

'Why?' said Paul, weakly.

'Let's not be silly about this, Mr Thomas, you have a box that doesn't belong to you, do you not?'

'What of it?'

'Well now, what of it indeed. We want it.'

'So do lots of people, it would seem,' said Paul.

'So you admit to having it?'

'You seem to know.'

'Yes, as I said, we have been watching you, Mr Thomas.'

'Would you mind telling me what this is all about?'

'Very well. I will tell you. But I caution you. If you allow the box into any hands other than ours, or tell anyone about it and its contents, you will be arrested and charged with treason.'

'Treason! That's absurd! I have done nothing of the sort.' Paul was now feeling frightened and had begun to sweat.

'As I said, Mr Thomas, if you allow the box to get into hands other than those of His Majesty's government, you will face serious consequences. So, please, hand it over.'

'How do I know you are genuine Secret Intelligence Service?'

'I showed you my ID.'

'That means nothing,' said Paul, thinking of all the fake IDs he had used in his career. 'The box is not here anyway. It is in a safe place. My house was broken into twice. I could not risk leaving it here.'

'You had better get it, Mr Thomas, we'll be back.'

To Paul's great surprise and relief, the two men left and he watched them drive away in a black Jaguar F-Pace, scattering gravel as they accelerated.

'MI6, my eye!' said Paul out loud. But he was worried. Suppose they were MI6, what's that, military intelligence involving overseas threats to the United Kingdom? How had they found out about the box?

Still unsure about going to the police, he decided to try to find out a little more about Herr Rasanov. Maybe he should be thinking of him as Comrade Rasanov. He had been thinking all along that he was dealing with Germans and somehow that was easier than if it was Russians he was up against. Germans are like us, he reasoned – but Russians – they are very different.

He needed to get the letters translated. Clive said he knew people at Cambridge who would be able to read Russian – if indeed it was Russian. He decided to risk emailing the photos of the documents to Clive.

He sent the email and sat thinking about his two visitors. Were they really MI6? Possibly, but unlikely. He had only caught a glimpse of their IDs and as he knew from personal experience, IDs are not reliable, he had used false IDs pretty much all his working life. No, he concluded, they were imposters.

If only he could find out who Henry had wanted the box to go to. He could hand it over and be done with it. Ask the guys at the club again if they knew Henry and if he had a wife. He had definitely said his wife. Perhaps he wasn't gay. Some men like to dress extravagantly, and Henry was a theatrical type. He thought of people who might be thought gay by their behaviour and dress, there were lots on television, who was that designer chap? Llewellyn something, he has a family but he acts gay. Henry has a wife, he concluded. But how to find her. He thought the woman claiming to be his wife was also an imposter.

Just as he was thinking how to find Henry's real wife, Clive rang.

'Hi, Paul Thomas', he said, cheerfully, 'I got your email. I have rung my friend at King's College. They do modern languages, so there's bound to be someone who can read the letters. I'll let you know as soon as I hear. You OK?'

'Yes, thanks, or will be when all this is over. It's getting me down. How are you? Recovered?'

'I'm absolutely fine, thanks. Bye then.'

'Bye, Clive, thanks.'

What a good friend Clive had turned out to be, he thought. Pity we lost touch. Never mind, plenty of time to catch up. He thought of those lovely vintage cars in Clive's collection. Maybe he would be able to drive some of them.

24

It was only two days later when Clive rang again.

'Hi, Paul, how are you doing? Check your email. I've attached a translation. My friend Andrew, well he's the son of a friend actually, who's studying at King's, got one of the professors to have a look at your letters. He was somewhat alarmed by the content and suggested you contact the police, but he has translated some of them. See what you think, OK. Must dash - I'm on the car phone. Talk soon, Bye now.'

Hastily thanking Clive, he could not wait to see what the professor had been able to make of the material he had photographed in Rasanov's safe.

Excited and not a little worried, Paul opened up his laptop.

Clive's email was one of many, mostly advertising. He opened it. Attached were copies of the letters and the reply from the Cambridge professor.

Dear Friend,

Herewith my best effort at translating the letters you sent me. Some of the technical terms were not familiar I'm afraid, but I think you will get the gist.
Военный Исследование Институт Can be translated as Military Research Institute. The address, Byelonovski, I am not familiar with. Letter reads as follows-

Dear Comrade Rasanov,
I have read with interest your findings in connection with lasers using rare elements. As you know we are developing lasers for military applications and have already experimented with some of the metals you suggest with moderate success.
I would be very pleased if you let me have the samples you mention. Even very tiny samples can be used in lasers as you know. So far we have used (here I could not translate) *and the results were promising. A target at one hundred meters was significantly damaged. We think we are on track with a weapon that could be used even against satellites if we can improve the range.*
So, my friend, please send your specimens as soon as possible.
Your friend,

(I could not read the signature – it looked a little like Kr...v..ski
The reply is simply agreeing to send the specimens as soon as they arrive from Spain by courier.
The other pages contained technical data which was beyond my linguistic capabilities. I am sorry. I hope I have

been of some help. But, please be careful. This material should be handed over to the appropriate authority.

Sincerely,

Robin Trenchingham-Gault

'Wow!' said Paul, still thinking aloud, 'weapons, perhaps those guys were MI6.'

Paul sat in his favourite chair in the living room to think what he should do. This box was clearly much more important and dangerous than he had thought. Had Henry been involved in this business with the Russians? Who was the mysterious wife to whom he was supposed to hand over the box? Where did the man on the motorbike fit in? Who were the people in Spain? Were they Russian spies? And why did they use an innocent man, me, to move the box into the UK? Why couldn't they send it straight to the Russians? And again, who was the woman claiming to be Henry's wife? She seemed to be the key. The questions went round and round in Paul's head until he had a headache and had to go in search of painkillers.

'Oh, God!' he exclaimed, with feeling. What am I going to do?' He feared that if he admitted having the box, he would be in all kinds of trouble, from whichever of the people involved. 'Perhaps I should just chuck it in the sea?' That idea appealed to him; the box contained material that could potentially be used against the UK. But the authorities needed to be made aware of this. He couldn't go to the police, they wouldn't believe him, they never did, and he would probably end up in prison for smuggling. He was uneasy about the secret services, they were scary, and the result would probably be the same, or worse. He didn't like to think of that. He had seen too many Bond films.

Could he somehow hand over the box anonymously? But then, whichever of the claimants he didn't give the box to, would be after him. He tried desperately to think which of his friends and acquaintances he could ask for advice. He didn't think any of the car club guys would be any help. There must be people in the publishing world, but he had lost touch with most of them. What about Jeremy Fosdyke, the editor of the magazine he had done most of his work for? He had always admired the man's great depth of knowledge. He tried to think if he had written any articles involving foreign agents. He'd come across plenty of foreigners, but most of them had been either criminals or victims of crimes that he had investigated. None of them, he thought were spies or anything like that, but then, if they were good spies, they would not give away their nefarious activities – he could have been involved with spies without ever suspecting. He

181

dismissed this train of thought, but it still hung there, just out of reach.

'Think, man, there must be somebody.' He was thinking aloud again.

Put it to Jeremy as an idea for an article, without disclosing too much. Yes, that's it!

He jotted down some bullet points before composing an email to his old editor. He hoped it would be enough to pique Jeremy's interest.

Hesitating for a moment he pressed 'send'.

25

Nothing happened for the next few days. Paul was on edge, expecting trouble.

The phone rang, making him almost jump out of his skin. He was shaking when he picked up the handset.

'Hello,' he didn't say, as he usually did, 'Paul Thomas, Hildisham 5924.'

'Hello, Paul, it's Jeremy, are you all right?'

'Oh, hello, Jeremy, yes, well no, actually. What do you think about the story?'

'You had me worried – is this real, or your imagination?'

Jeremy had clearly seen through his subterfuge, and realised Paul's idea for a story was more than met the eye.

'You guessed; it is real I'm afraid. I didn't know who to go to for advice. What do you think?'

'You'll have to tell me more, why don't you come to the office?'

'Oh, OK, I suppose I could. Do you think you might be able to help me?'

'I will if I can, old man, you know me. Come as soon as you can.'

Paul was sure Jeremy was one of the good guys and he needed to confide in someone, so he decided to go down to London straight away.

Reluctantly leaving the car in the station car park at Cromer Station, he boarded the train for first part of the journey, as far as Norwich. Although he quite enjoyed train travel, Paul was finding it a chore.

At last arriving at Liverpool Street Station, he decided to take a taxi to Crane Court, off Fleet Street, where Topical Magazines had their offices.

He announced himself to the young woman on reception, she was not one he had seen before. He imagined turnover was quite frequent. She told him to go straight through to Mr Fosdyke's office on the first floor.

Jeremy greeted him with his usual firm handshake and bade him sit.

'Coffee?' he asked.

It took quite a while for Paul to tell the whole story right from the beginning and Jeremy listened intently without interrupting.

'It's quite a story, old man, but much as I like it, not one that we could run. I'm sorry. I think it's one for the big guys round the corner.' Jeremy said when

Paul had finished, meaning the newspapers in Fleet Street.

'I wasn't actually thinking of offering it, Jeremy. I need your advice.'

'Oh, but you do intend to write it, surely? You will get a good price in the street. Any of the big ones would love to run it.'

'Perhaps, when it's all over, but right now it is too dangerous. I was hoping you might offer me some advice.'

'I see what you mean about being dangerous – it's red hot. But other than going to press with it, I don't know. Really. I am sorry, old man.' He sat back in his executive chair and steepled his hands. 'Have some more coffee?'

Paul was disappointed. He thought Jeremy, with his experience in political journalism, would be able to offer a solution. He accepted the coffee, but then bade the man good bye. He would have to think of something else.

Thinking that his journey had been a waste of time, he walked along Fleet Street admiring as always, the wonderful view of Sir Christopher Wren's masterpiece at the top of Ludgate Hill.

He became aware of someone following him. He had seen the man several times since arriving at Liverpool Street. He had lost him when he took the taxi, but he spotted him again when he left the magazine offices. He passed Ye Olde Cheshire Cheese and risked a glance behind him. He was still there. Past Itsu Japanese restaurant, across Farringdon Street onto Ludgate Hill, St Paul's looming magnificently. He stopped outside Association Coffee and considered going in, but then, spotting the entrance to London Thameslink, he dodged traffic and crossed as quickly as he could and ducked into the station, hoping there would be crowds in which to lose himself. There weren't. The place was deserted. Not daring to look round he had to decide what to do. He opted to head for Luton. If the man still followed him, he could be sure. No coincidence could see anyone else heading for Luton from his publishers.

On the station platform, the man was only five or six yards away. He was dressed in a dark blue suit with a red tie. He carried the obligatory umbrella, like a typical London businessman. He had a very severe haircut, the style popular with American servicemen. His shoes were plain Oxfords. There really was nothing remarkable about him except for the worrying fact that he was following Paul. To Paul, he looked dangerous, menacing even, and he was worried.

When the train arrived Paul tried to get into a different carriage, but the mystery man was close behind.

There were very few people on the train and it was impossible to get away from his pursuer. Acting more boldly than he felt, he approached the man.

'What do you want? Why are you following me?'

'Have you got it?'

'What are you talking about.'

'Have you got it?'

'I'm sorry, you are confusing me with someone else.'

'I know exactly who I'm talking to, Mr Thomas. Have you got it?'

'No, I haven't. Who are you anyway?'

The man showed his ID long enough for Paul to read it. It had an embossed United States bald eagle emblem with Central Intelligence Agency in raised letters round it on one side and a photograph and the name, Agent Joseph T. Hennessy on the other side. He snapped it shut and put it away.

'CIA! Exclaimed Paul. For goodness' sake, it will be the KGB next.'

'Do not jest, Mr Thomas, it probably will be. I doubt they are far behind. It would safer to give it to me'

'What has it to do with America?' Paul asked.

'Everything has to do with America ultimately. Now just hand it over and you can forget all about it.'

Paul was feeling very frightened. His knees suddenly felt weak and he sat down. He wished he had never set eyes on Henry Cartingdon-Bligh and his parcel. He was being pursued by criminals, terrorists and government agents. What on earth could he do? He sat with his head in his hands in utter despair.

He could not sit long – the CIA agent was demanding him to hand over the package. And what's more he was pointing a gun at him. It was a nasty looking Glock 17 or 19. He couldn't see exactly which as the weapons are very similar. When one is pointed at your head it doesn't really matter which.

'For goodness' sake, if you shoot me, you will never find the box.' Paul tried to sound braver than he felt.

The agent lowered his gun. 'I could shoot you in the foot. It would hurt like hell and then you would tell me.' He laughed.

'Look, all I can tell you is that several people want the box. Some of them I suspect have intentions for its contents that your government would not approve of. The British secret services also want the box, for the same reason. Why don't you get together with MI6 and work out a plan that would ensure the box remains in safe hands?' Paul looked hopefully at the CIA man, who was still pointing his gun at his feet.

The man didn't reply, but replaced the gun in its holster somewhere near his armpit. Paul felt more comfortable.

'So, what do you say? Good idea?'

'Ah don't rightly know. I have never dealt with your secret service guys. Would they cooperate with the US of A? It might be worth a try at that. Better than shooting you, anyway.' He laughed again, and poked Paul in the ribs, almost friendly.

'How would I get in touch with your guy? What's his name?'

'He's not my guy. He wasn't even as friendly as you, although he didn't threaten to shoot me. I don't know how you would find him, but he's sure to show up before long.'

'Where did you say the box is hidden?' CIA man asked suddenly.

'You won't catch me like that. It stays hidden until some solution is agreed.'

'Where are you headed? Home? Where is that?' asked the man in quick succession.

'Well, I was trying to get away from you and took the first train available. It's going to Luton and it will be there soon. I actually live in Norfolk, so I'll have to find another train.'

'You did a good job avoiding me as long as you did, I must say. Have you done this sort of thing before? Say, you ain't security service are you?'

'No, certainly not. I am retired now. I was a journalist. I've been in a few scrapes in my time.'

'Man like you could be useful to us. How about working for Uncle Sam? The pay's good.'

It was Paul's turn to laugh, but the man seemed serious. He didn't know what to say. A few years ago the proposition might have been attractive. He didn't reply.

An announcement on the train's tannoy warned that they were due to arrive at Luton Parkway in five minutes.

'Are you going to allow me to continue my journey, Mr CIA?' said Paul.

'My name is Joseph T Hennessy, I showed you, my card. You can call me Agent Hennessy.'

'Gee, thanks,' said Paul, trying to emulate the man's accent. 'So what are you going to do? Agent Hennessy.'

'I'll just string along with you. I'll keep out sight if you prefer.'

'That would be wise,' said Paul.

'Just pretend you don't know me.'

'That won't be difficult.'

When the train drew into the station the two men disembarked a few feet from each other and made for the ticket office.

Paul was surprised to discover how many trains went to Norwich. And was not unhappy with the fare of forty pounds for the three-hour journey. Ignoring the CIA man, he headed for the platform.

If he had hoped to lose the man, he was disappointed, out of the corner of his eye, he saw the man heading his way.

He was surprised to find that there were frequent trains from Norwich to Cromer and the forty-minute journey would only cost nine pounds.

Paul lost sight of his pursuer in Cromer station. He could not be sure, but hoped he had eluded him. By now he was desperate to get home and could not wait to get to Cromer, where he'd parked the car.

Even though the roads were not as good on the coast road, he chose to go that way, simply because he liked it. There was not much in it for time.

26

Exhausted after his fruitless meeting with the editor and his encounter with the CIA man, Paul flopped down in his armchair as soon as he got back home. He wanted a cup of coffee but didn't have the energy to get it. He simply sat, thinking over the events of the day.

'Where is it going to end?' he said to himself. This was proving to be one of the most difficult situations he'd been in. Not so much physical danger, although there had been that, too, but this was having a devastating effect on him mentally. He was worried sick about being the target of so many unpleasant people. He was going to have to give up the box to someone – but who?

Much as he disliked involving the police with his problems, he was quickly coming to the conclusion that he must consult them.

After maybe twenty minutes, he got up and went into the kitchen to make coffee. It would have to be instant as he could not be bothered with the process of making what he called proper coffee.

He was very tempted to add a slug of Jameson's to the black liquid, but he resisted and put two spoonfulls of brown sugar in instead.

A pile of mail had appeared on his mat, and although he was sure there would be nothing of interest, he gathered it up and took it back to his chair.

'Better than no mail at all I suppose', he muttered to himself. At least someone acknowledges my existence beside agents from foreign countries. Despite everything, he smiled.

Most of the envelopes were indeed uninteresting but one, that didn't have a stamp, looked ominous.

He tore it open nervously. In crude handwritten capital letters were written – THE BOX – OR ELSE TONIGHT. DO NOT IGNORE THIS.

Paul felt a chill down his back and he began to sweat. His hands shook. There was no indication who had sent the message. He suspected Rasanov because he would not have expected either MI6 or the CIA to resort to such methods.

'Right, that's it!' he said. 'The police, now.'

It would have to be Fakenham police, as there was only a one-man part-time station in Hildisham, and although it was late, he felt he could delay no longer.

Just as he was about to get in the car, a large black saloon drew up outside the house. Two men got out and approached him. He tried to ignore them and got into the car.

Before he could lock the door, one of the men wrenched it open and dragged him out and onto the ground. He lay on the wet gravel, looking up at the man who now was brandishing an automatic pistol in a most unfriendly fashion. Despite the situation, Paul was interested to note the man still favoured the Makarov PM. A sidearm that had largely been replaced according to people in the know.

'Get up!' demanded the man, and Paul scrambled to his feet.

'In the car!' said the other man, who also had a pistol in his hand.

'Who are you, what do you want?' Paul managed to say, despite his mouth suddenly becoming very dry.

'You come with us,' said the first man. Then he and his companion grabbed Paul and pushed him into the back of the car. The door slammed shut and the car drove off. Paul tried the door, bit it was locked. A glass screen divided the interior of the car so he was unable to speak to his captors. Futilely, he hammered on the glass. Angry more than afraid at first.

After banging on the glass for several minutes, it was clear to Paul that he was wasting his energy. He would just have to wait and hope for the best.

Paul was wishing he had gone to the police before. What was going to happen to him now? They would not kill him. They would never find the box. It must be the box they were after. But they might torture him. That's how the Russians worked, evidently.

After about an hour, the car stopped and reversed into a garage. Paul could not tell where they were. The windows of the car were heavily tinted so he hadn't been able to see where they were going.

'Out!' said the man, when he opened the door. Paul had no choice and didn't want to be manhandled again. 'This way!' said the man. He was not pointing his pistol now. 'Thank goodness' thought Paul.

He was led into the kitchen of what appeared to be an ordinary house and told to sit on a kitchen chair.

'Now, Mister Thomas, we mean you no harm. Where is box?' The man's English was almost perfect, but not quite. He was almost certainly Russian thought Paul.

'Who are you?' asked Paul.

'Federal'naya sluzhba bezopasnosti Rossiyskoy Federatsii,' said the man.

'That means nothing to me,' said Paul.

'You know better, 'Komitet Gosudarst-vennoy Bezopasnosti? KGB,' said the man, smiling.

'Well, I've heard of that, obviously. What does the KGB want with me?'

'Is not KGB now. 'Federal'naya sluzhba bezopasnosti Rossiyskoy Federatsii, Security Agency of Russian Federation. You understand now?'

'I think so. What's your name?'

'Just call us Agent Boris and Agent Ivan,' said the man, smiling. They both gave a little bow.

'OK, so why me, what do you want with me?'

'You have box. Important to security of Russian Federation.'

'What makes you think I have it?'

'We know everything. Box was meant to be given to one of our agents, but you have it instead. You refuse to give to agent. Now you give it to us.'

'Do you mean to say that Henry – and his so-called wife are Russian agents?' Paul could hardly believe it.

'Of course.'

'But I've known Henry for years.'

'Yes, called sleeper, not until now needed.' Boris's English was slipping.

'So, where is box?'

'First tell me, are you working with the Germans?'

'Not Germans, Agent Rasanov. He also sleeper. We have many.' Boris smiled again.

'I happen to know what you intend to use the material in the box for,' said Paul, regretting it immediately.

'Oh!' said Ivan, sharply. 'How you know this?'

'I've been doing a little spying myself.'

'This is serious,' said Boris and turned to Ivan speaking rapidly in Russian.

'Oh, Lord, now what have I done?' thought Paul, 'why did you tell them that?'

The two agents, who had been quite calm, were now agitated.

'You come now,' said Ivan, grabbing Paul's arm and pulling him roughly.

'You go in cellar. Tell us where box.'

It took the two of them to force Paul down the steps into the cellar, but he was unable to resist. They left him and closed the door. He heard the lock click. It was dark and cold in the cellar.

There was a grille through which perhaps coal had once been delivered, and with the little light that filtered through, Paul was eventually able to explore his prison. He found a large cardboard box containing books, and sat down.

27

Paul was thinking of his conversation with the CIA man when he jokingly said it would be the KGB next. The agent had warned that that might well be true, but Paul had dismissed it as fanciful. Now he was faced with the dreadful reality. He was going to have to hand over the box knowing its contents could be used against the free world. Or, was he brave enough to resist, and become perhaps a dead hero. Could he endure torture? He very much doubted it. What would they do to him? 'God Help me!' he prayed, and he meant his prayer more than any prayer before, and there had been a few in times of danger. He had survived many dangerous situations, but these two Russians were the biggest threat he had ever faced, and he was very afraid.

He could measure the hours of his captivity with his watch as the hands crept slowly round, but it was the cycle of light and dark from the grille that enabled him to count the days. So this was their method, starvation and thirst.

He had already been thirsty when they put him in the cellar, now after two days, he was desperate for a drink. His tongue stuck to the roof of his mouth. He was hungry, but it was water he needed most. He knew he could go without food for days; he had done before, but not without water. He had an idea it was three days without water and three weeks without food. The rule of three they called it. Where had he heard that? It was cool in the cellar, so maybe he could manage four days. But surely they would not risk him dying – they needed the information.

He climbed the steps and banged on the door, shouting, 'water! I need water!' But to no avail.

He had read of people drinking their own urine. He looked around for a container of some sort. He found a tin lid. It was dirty, and he cleaned it as well as he could with his handkerchief, then, carefully urinated into it, spilling most of the contents of his bladder onto the floor. He tentatively put the tin lid to his lips. His urine stank, he shuddered and took a tiny sip. The taste was so awful he retched. That wouldn't do. He would vomit more liquid than he'd taken in.

Day three dawned. He had heard nothing from the Russians. They must give him a drink today, or they would risk not getting the information they needed.

He had been sleeping fitfully until a commotion above him caused him to wake up. Were they coming?

The noises above got louder and raised voices could be heard over the banging.

After a while it all went quiet. What's happening? They can't go away without him, or without giving him water. He would die.

There were no noises at all for several hours and Paul was certain his captors had gone. This then was it. He would die in this cellar. He thought about his life. He'd had a good innings, had some good times, married a wonderful woman, then lost her, but he'd had adventures, done things that most people only dreamed of.

He remembered the time when he and his friends Richard and Barbara had risked being burned alive in a flaming windmill, and he recalled the time when he'd been tied up in a dark cave but had escaped by attacking his captors.

He had travelled – not far beyond the UK, but widely within its islands, he had particularly enjoyed Scotland, and he'd had adventures on the sea and in the air, and he'd made some good friends. Not a bad life. But he was not ready to go, not just yet. He recalled his namesake, Dylan Thomas's poem – he'd studied Thomas at college and had

memorised this well- known poem. Despite his dry
mouth he recited it aloud.

Do not go gentle into that good night,
Old age should burn and rave at close of day;
Rage, rage against the dying of the light.
Though wise men at their end know dark is right,
Because their words had forked no lightning they
Do not go gentle into that good night.
Good men, the last wave by, crying how bright
Their frail deeds might have danced in a green bay,
Rage, rage against the dying of the light.
Wild men who caught and sang the sun in flight,
And learn, too late, they grieved it on its way,
Do not go gentle into that good night.
Grave men, near death, who see with blinding sight
Blind eyes could blaze like meteors and be gay,
Rage, rage against the dying of the light.
And you, my father, there on the sad height,
Curse, bless me now with your fierce tears, I pray.
Do not go gentle into that good night.
Rage, rage against the dying of the light.

It was some hours later that he heard movements
above him again and the door opened, letting in
light which momentarily blinded him.

'Hello! Are you all right? Mr Thomas, is it?' A
gruff but friendly voice as a large figure descended
the steps. It was a uniformed policeman, a sergeant

201

in fact. He looked at Paul with kindly eyes and Paul could have cried, but no tears would come.

'Oh, thank you!' he croaked. 'I need water, please.'

Too weak, at first, to be taken from his prison, Paul had been given water and urged to sip it slowly, and then when he felt a little better, the sergeant had somehow found sandwiches. An hour or so later, Paul was helped up the steps.

The house appeared to be full of people. He recognised the MI6 agent and the CIA man, and there were several uniformed policemen and others he took to be detectives. It was one of these that addressed him.

'Mr Thomas, my name is Chief Inspector Grant, Special Branch. I am so pleased we found you. Can you tell us what happened?'

'It's a very long story, and one I'll gladly tell, but not just yet. I need to recover. It's all too much at the moment.'

'I understand of course, but you do realise that it is important we find out as quickly as possible, the facts of this case.'

'This case,' thought Paul. 'Yes, I do, Chief Inspector, I do.'

Paul was led outside where several cars were lined up at the curb. He got into one of the cars, a black Jaguar XF. To his utter amazement, there sat Clive, with the biggest grin on his face.

'How did you get here? Paul asked.

'It's a long story,' Clive said.

'Aren't they all!' said Paul, laughing and shaking his friend's hand enthusiastically.

When all the stories had been told and retold to police and various government agencies, it had been possible to piece together the whole affair.

Long before Paul's involvement, MI6 and the CIA knew about the potential use of some rare metals in weaponry. They knew that there were samples of very rare and valuable minerals in the collection of an amateur geologist who had been collecting them simply for his own interest. But before they could get hold of them, someone had got wind of them and stolen them. The box of samples found its way to Spain; agents of the Russian Federation had then obtained it, realising its significance. The trail had then gone cold. It was only later that the German firm, that specialised in rare metals, got wind of the samples and wanted them for their research, and in turn another Russian agent working for the firm had found out about them and had entered the chase.

When Henry, a Russian 'sleeper' according to Agent Boris, had obtained the box, he had intended to take it personally to the woman who claimed to be his wife. She in turn would have handed it over to her superiors. But because of Henry's illness, Paul had been given custody of the samples, having no idea until later of their value. Thankfully he had not been tempted enough to hand them over to any of the protagonists.

Clive had been about to call on Paul when he saw the Russians take him away. He didn't of course know who these men were, only that they had his friend and he had to do something. At precisely that moment another car drove up and the MI6 man got out demanding to know what Clive was doing and where was Paul Thomas. Clive told him all he knew and they both set off in pursuit of the Russians.

The CIA agent, last on the scene of course, stumbled upon the MI6 man and Clive and joined the party. The two agents argued about whose case this was and had to report back to their respective units.

In the meantime, Clive, who had continued to follow the Russians' car, had seen the car drive into the garage of a suburban house. He had hidden and watched, but eventually, not knowing what to do, he did what Paul should have done in the first place, he told the police. Special Branch had been alerted and things quickly began to happen.

The whereabouts of the box of samples was now the question all parties were asking.

Paul was not happy for any of the agencies to get hold of the samples for fear they would be used to develop deadly weapons. He stalled. He claimed he could not remember what he'd done with them, but of course they didn't believe that.

He was taken to his house, along with several cars full of policemen and agents. When they arrived at Fishers' Lane, they all began to argue, and in the confusion, Paul was able to slip into the house and retrieve the box from its hiding place in the chimney where it had been all along, and spill its contents amongst the ashes from his wood burner. He carefully crushed the little glass containers with a poker and mixed all the samples in the ash so that they could not be identified.

When it came to handing over the box, he said he thought one or other of the string of people that had handled the box must have taken them, or lost them.

It was impossible to disprove Paul's explanation, and if truth be known, most of the people involved were pleased to know the samples were no more.

The Russian agents, including Rasanov, had been taken into custody and would no doubt be exchanged at some point for agents of the West.

When Paul was fully recovered from his ordeal, he returned to Cambridgeshire and spent a long time happily playing with Clive's collection of vehicles and drinking Doom Bar in the local pub.

'You know, Clive,' Paul said after an enjoyable day, 'I really am going to retire. Absolutely no more adventures.' He raised his glass. 'Cheers.'